FRONTIER JUSTICE

Book One:
Yellow Knife

FRONTIER JUSTICE

Book One:
Yellow Knife

•

DON HEPLER

AVALON BOOKS
THOMAS BOUREGY AND COMPANY, INC.
401 LAFAYETTE STREET
NEW YORK, NEW YORK 10003

PRINTED IN THE UNITED STATES OF AMERICA
ON ACID-FREE PAPER
BY HADDON CRAFTSMEN, SCRANTON, PENNSYLVANIA

FRONTIER JUSTICE

Book One:
Yellow Knife

60,483

Chapter One

Rebecca lay quiet in the box and peered through the small crack at the men who had just killed her family. There were five of them, ragged and dirty, and they had been very businesslike and thorough.

Father had said hello and they had not even bothered talking to him. The one with the crooked arm had simply pulled his pistol and shot into Father three times. Mom had let out a small scream of shock and horror, and the bald one had pulled his pistol and said, "Don't do that, Ma'am." Whatever he hadn't wanted Mother to do she had gone ahead and done, raised the shotgun probably, and he had shot her one time. And that was how her family had died.

It had happened so fast that it didn't seem real to her yet. It was hard to believe that Father and Mother were lying above her with the life blasted out of them. It was much too awful for a fifteen-year-old girl to comprehend, and so she lay quiet in the box. Lay quiet and waited to see what would happen next.

Father had built the box himself, adding it under the wagon. Blending it in under there so it wasn't something a body would notice right away. He had built it big enough for her and Mother, only when the strangers had shown on the horizon, Mother had chosen to stay out with him even though he had tried to send her into the box with Rebecca. He had built it with the idea that they could hide in it in the event of Indian attack, only it had not been Indians but rather men of their own like who had proved to be the real savages.

The five men sat on their horses for a long minute looking at what they had just done, and Rebecca made herself look at them hard, made herself imprint their likeness in her mind before they slowly dismounted.

"That seems like a real shame," said the one wearing an old Confederate uniform jacket. He walked around the front of the wagon and out of her view.

"I told her not to do that," whined the balding one who had shot her mother. "You want I should have let her shoot me?"

The next was a hard-looking young man with wild yellowish hair, and he laughed, weird and harsh. His laugh was a little too harsh, a little too tight, and it reminded Rebecca of Walter Krone back home. Walter had been not quite right in the head, an embarrassment to his parents and prone to do shocking things and then laugh about them. Like the time he took off all his clothes and walked into the general store for some new ones.

The young man ran his dirty hand through his wild hair with no apparent result. "If she had shot you there would have been more for the rest of us," he said. The balding one looked annoyed.

"I do get tired of you riding me all the time, boy," the balding one said. He paused and looked at the wild-headed one long and seriously. "Some day I may have to put a hole in you," he finally finished.

"I'm so scared I am shaking all over," the boy said back, followed by that same strange laugh. He walked toward the back of the wagon, limping badly. In a moment Rebecca heard and felt the back gate slam down.

The fourth man was older, with wrinkles creasing deep in his face. Not that he was past his prime, just that he had done some hard living, most of it out of doors. He took off his dirty hat and wiped his forehead with his forearm. Seemed funny that he should be sweating when it was so cool.

"I told you no killing, didn't I?" he said, voice tight with anger.

"Hey, Jubil," whined the last one, the one with the crooked arm who had shot her Father. "I heard you tell us that. I didn't want to shoot him. He was going for a gun.'' The older man looked disgusted.

"Don't give me that, Amos,'' he said. "Don't you lie to me like you think I am stupid or something, you hear?''

"I don't think you are stupid, Jubil,'' Crooked Arm said, and Rebecca could easily hear the fear in his voice. "I thought he was going for a gun. Honest.''

Jubil turned away from him and walked to the rear of the wagon.

"You are a liar, Amos,'' he said calmly, "and the next time you do not listen to me I will kill you dead.'' Now they were all out of her sight and she lay there and listened as they rummaged through the wagon only inches above her.

She did not think they would discover her. The cover was closed and bolted, and it blended in with the wagon floor so nobody would ever suspect it was there. All she had to do was stay quiet until they were gone. She tried to keep her breathing as silent as possible, tried not to think about the only two people in the world she had loved, now lying dead.

She heard the stuff of their home being dragged out of the wagon and dropped carelessly to the ground. Mother had so loved some of those things, and it made her angry to have those dirty-handed strangers pawing through their belongings. As the hour wore on, she listened to them bickering about who got to keep things that were rightfully not theirs, and anger gradually replaced her fear. She would get even. Someday. Somehow. She would find them and she would get even. They would pay for callously killing Mother and Father. Pay hard, so they would have time to regret what they did to her family. What they did to her.

"Let's camp right here," said Confederate Jacket.

"Now there's a real intelligent idea," from Jubil. "Let us hang around here until somebody comes and discovers what you morons have done and then we can really 'hang' around here."

"And you think *I* am stupid," said Amos to Jubil.

"Yes I do," said Jubil, and the kid with the limp laughed his awful cackle.

"Gather up their horses," said Jubil, "and let us get away from here." The sounds of harness being removed, dropped, and then slaps and the horses trotted off.

They came back into her view and Rebecca watched them swing back into their saddles, all of them with some of her family's belongings tied on behind. She could see their quilts and blankets, some of Father's clothing and even one of Mother's fine Sunday bonnets. They turned and kicked their horses into motion, her family's four horses trailing behind.

"Four horses, thirty-two dollars, some clothes and blankets," Jubil said. "Their lives weren't worth much."

"Hey, I said I was sorry," whined Amos. "Besides, better them than us."

"Shut up, Amos," said Jubil.

"Okay, Jubil," Amos said. "I'm shutting up." The sounds of the horses faded into the distance, and soon only the soft cold wind remained.

"I have been thinking on giving up this profession," Wiley said as he drew a bead on the spot where the Indian had vanished. His rifle blasted and the recoil slammed against his shoulder. A puff of dust rising from the prairie grass clearly told him that the Indian had moved and his shot was wasted. He levered another shell into the chamber and looked down the barrel, waiting for a target to present itself. "I am not quite sure what profession I should get into, though," he went on in a conversational tone. "Any ideas?"

His companion, lying beside him in the swale, never took his eyes off the prairie to their front. "Whatever it is," he said, "it shouldn't involve any serious shooting." Wiley, of course, took offense right away.

"If you are referring to that last shot," he said indignantly, "I could have hit him if I wanted. I just figured on scaring him, that's all."

"You figured on scaring a Sioux?"

"Only seems fair," Wiley came back. "They are sure scaring me." His friend smiled.

"Me, too," he said. He studied the prairie. If a body didn't know for sure there were six or seven men out there, he'd swear there was nothing. Grass wasn't that long either, and it was hard to believe that full-grown men could disappear so completely. 'Course these weren't normal men. They were Indians, Sioux probably, and they had a habit of doing what was hard to believe.

"So how do you figure it?" Wiley asked.

"They want our horses and guns, o' course," Nest came back. "Way I see it, they are working on surrounding us while we are lying here resting."

"Yup," Wiley said with a long sigh. "That's just about what I thought." He rolled over on his back so he could watch behind them. Their two horses and pack horse chomped the dry prairie grass contentedly, not caring that they would very likely be wearing paint and feathers for the rest of their horsey lives. "Don't suppose they will get tired and go home?" he went on.

"Prob'ly will," said his friend. "Right after they are finished killing us."

"I think I will become a clerk," said Wiley, as though he hadn't heard his friend. "Maybe in Patterson's General Store. I believe I could sell things to the women in town. Or maybe I could go to a big city and work in the library. Lot of quiet in a library, you know." His friend didn't respond, so Wiley glanced over at him.

Nest was studying on the prairie to his front, trying to find a target for his Winchester. There was a place out there where the grass looked a little shorter than the rest and he was reasonably certain there was a very healthy and rather irritated Indian in that particular spot. He toyed with the idea of slapping a shot out there, but decided to wait for a little more confirmation before wasting a round. He adjusted his position slightly because his badge was digging into his chest.

"Don't think you will make it as a storekeeper," he finally said.

"Why not?"

"Take you a month or so just to learn the trade," Nest came back. "That seems a little excessive since it does not appear you have that much left in your natural life span."

"You do not have a very hopeful outlook," Wiley observed, "especially where I am concerned."

"You forget I have seen you shoot," Nest said.

In spite of himself, Wiley chuckled. "Not funny," he said through his smile.

"No offense," from Nest. He straightened up a little. "I think we are about to be rescued," he said, amazement clear in his voice. Wiley rolled over and looked in the same direction as his friend.

Yellow Knife heard the footsteps coming long before he could see anything. He was quite earnestly engaged in making himself as small a target as possible, willing himself to become part of the earth itself. Those two men were armed with long guns, and they were not slow about using them. Three Fingers was already hurt and maybe dead, and Yellow Knife did not see any reason to hurry and join him. His first time out with a hunting party had not quite turned out the way he had imagined.

At first it had been wild and exciting, chasing the white men across the prairie, hair flying in the wind and his horse running beneath him. Then they had taken to ground and one of them had shot Three Fingers with his long gun and Yellow Knife had been shocked at the raw power a single bullet had. Three Fingers had flown into the air when the bullet hit him in the front of his shoulder, and when he came down and fell to the ground there was a large area of torn meat on his back where the bullet had gone out of him and his blood was running out like water.

And so he stayed motionless as the footsteps approached, trusting that he was very hard to see as long as he didn't move. The feet crunched closer and closer, crushing the dry fall grass under their tread, and he held his knife and waited to see what life had in store for him next. The feet were coming right toward him. They stepped up close by the side of his head and stopped. They were so close, so close. Yellow Knife didn't know whether to stay still or look. Curiosity won out. He turned his head very slowly until he could look up at the intruder.

It was a young white girl, and she was standing there looking down on him, confusion plain in her eyes. She was carrying a very large pistol in her hand, but it was hanging straight at her side, pointing harmlessly at the ground. They contemplated each other seriously for a long moment.

Yellow Knife really had no desire to harm the young girl, but he felt he should do *something*, so he moved his knife hand slowly forward. The girl matched his movement, raising the pistol until it pointed at his head. He moved his hand back where it had been before and she let the pistol hang down once more.

This was humiliating. He knew he should do something but he didn't know what. This young girl had stumbled upon him, and he lay there like a foolish boy while she had him at her mercy. He closed his eyes and turned his face back down to the ground. They would laugh at him around the fire tonight. If she let him live.

In a minute, she walked on.

"Over here, girl!" called Nest. The girl looked over at where he was waving to her, hesitated a moment, then walked to where the two men were huddled in the swale.

"Hello," she said in a conversational tone.

"Come down here, girl," said Nest urgently. "There's Indians about." The girl casually walked down into the ditch.

"They must be gone," Wiley said to his friend. "Else they never would have let her come walking in here like that."

"They are still out there," she said. "I almost

stepped on one of them.'' She didn't seem overly concerned.

''You almost stepped on one of them?'' Wiley repeated dumbly.

''Yes,'' she said. ''I thought at first he was going to do something because he moved his knife, but when I pointed Father's pistol at him, he settled down and looked away like I wasn't even there.'' Nest rolled on his side and studied on the girl for a moment.

She was little more than a child, maybe fifteen years old. She had pale gray eyes that peered out somberly from beneath her gay blue bonnet. Her dress matched her bonnet and the only thing out of place on her was the big Walker Colt she was carrying in her right hand. She looked back at him calmly.

''You know how to shoot that thing?'' he asked.

''I have never really shot it,'' she said somewhat defensively, ''but I know how to do it. You just pull back the hammer and aim it and squeeze the trigger. I saw Father do it once.'' He grunted and turned his attention back to the front. Nothing moved out there.

''Where is your father?'' Nest asked. When there was no answer right away, he glanced over at the girl. Her expression was tight, almost haggard, but her eyes shone with inner anger.

''He is dead,'' she said, looking him right in the eye. ''He was killed for thirty-two dollars, four horses, and some blankets and clothes. He and Mother are

back that way"—she pointed one small hand—
"about half a day's walk."

"Indians get 'em?" Wiley asked without taking his
eyes from the prairie in front of him.

"White men," she said. "Five white men."

"How long ago?" from Nest.

"It was not yet mid-morning when they came up
on us. Father sent me into the hiding box before they
saw me, and they never knew I was there. That is why
I am not dead like my folks."

"What's your name, girl?" Nest asked.

"Rebecca Ward."

"You come on over here and lay down beside me,"
he said. "We are lawmen and will go back and bury
your parents and hunt for the villains as soon as we
get over this little piece of Indian trouble we are pres-
ently involved in."

"You are lawmen?" she asked. Nest rolled over so
she could see his badge.

Satisfied, she nodded, walked casually over to him,
and carefully lay down on the grassy bank beside him.
It was obvious she did not want to get her dress dirty,
and Nest figured that maybe she had put on her best
outfit before she began walking into the prairie . . . into
the unknown. He glanced over at her and she stared
back somberly.

"My name is Nestor, Rebecca," he said. "It is a
good thing you stumbled on us on account of you are
heading west and it is a long way to the next town."

"I was not looking for a town, Mr. Nest," she said, matter-of-fact. "I was looking for the men who killed my parents. It was my intention to shoot them with Father's pistol." Nest looked into her steady gray eyes, impressed in spite of himself.

"You are long on courage, Becky," he said. "Long on courage and just a little short on good sense. You would have likely died out here, and even if you had found the men you seek, they would have killed you."

"I prefer to be called Rebecca," she said, then, "I am not as foolish as you might think, Mr. Nest. You appear to be the one in danger. I was doing just fine, thank you."

"For someone whose life I am saving, you are certainly a snippy little thing," Nest observed. "And I prefer to be called Nest, if you please," he mimicked her voice. Her gray eyes hardened with anger and he could see there was a temper there.

"Listen, people," said Wiley. "If you could maybe finish your conversation later, I believe they are up to something out there."

Nest snapped his attention out to the front and thumbed back the hammer on his rifle. Sure enough, he could see movement in the grass, but for the life of him, he could not see any sign of an Indian.

Yellow Knife felt Crooked Fist tug on his foot and looked over at him. He had not heard Crooked Fist coming at all, and he was impressed with his friend's prowess. Crooked Fist was grinning at him.

"How do you like your first battle?" Crooked Fist asked.

"Better than Three Fingers, I think," Yellow Knife said. Crooked Fist's grin disappeared.

"He is dead," he said. "I do not wish to be the one to tell his wife." Three Fingers's wife was a large woman, loud of voice, with the temper and disposition of a cornered coyote. She would not take news of his death well, and would doubtless blame the messenger. Yellow Knife believed that no matter how bad it was, Three Fingers was better off dead. The others would miss his clowning, however.

"If we finish this," Crooked Fist said, "More of us will die. These men shoot well." Yellow Knife waited to hear the decision of his friend.

"Why did you let the girl go free?" Crooked Fist asked. Yellow Knife had been dreading the question.

"I do not make war on little girls," he said. It was a good answer.

"Especially little girls with big handguns," Crooked Fist observed with a trace of humor. Yellow Knife looked back at his friend. It was going to be as bad as he thought. Crooked Fist had seen everything, and Crooked Fist was a good storyteller. Everyone would know. Still, it was better to be the butt of jokes for a little while than to be dead forever.

"I think we should go away and live to fight another

day," said Crooked Fist. "I would truly like to have one of those rifles for my own," he added wistfully.

He turned and slithered away. Yellow Knife followed.

Chapter Two

Mary Allen had met Walt in New York City. He had seemed clean-cut and hardworking and he claimed to love her very much, so she had married him. Life had been hard but good, and when Walt told her he wanted to seek his fortune on the frontier she had actually been excited by the prospect of great adventure. So they went west, finally settling in Kansas where Walt had built a small house of sod sliced from the living prairie.

The house itself had provided enough adventure for Mary. When the sod was ripped from the prairie, all the former tenants had come along with it, and there was never a shortage of insect life in the dark interior of the home, not to mention the occasional snake that dropped from the ceiling and scared her half out of her wits. Naturally, there was always a fine layer of dust that filtered down, and cleanliness was next to God sure enough, but it was also next to impossible.

There were plenty of good memories to go along with the bad, and their son Nestor was far and away the best. They had produced three sons, but Nestor was the only one to make it to adulthood. Robert had died in the spring of his eighth year, died trying to get away from the fierce pain low on his side. His fever kept getting worse and worse, and then one day Mary knew he would not live and he hadn't lasted until nightfall. He had been a wonderful boy, bright and happy, and they buried him out there and marked the grave with a wooden cross. His brother lay beside him, stillborn and unnamed, and Mary had tended the graves until Walt took sick and died. She had buried him with his sons and come into town, for by then there was a town, such as it was.

Ralph Peterson had paid her cash money for her farm, and Mary had bought her house, a fine structure made of wood, and taken in boarders to help make ends meet. She knew Ralph was now growing crops over her two sons and Walt, but somehow she didn't think that was a bad thing; didn't think Walt would mind, or the boys either.

Nestor had taken a liking to the town marshal, and the marshal took a liking to Nestor and they spent considerable time together, a fact that at first had not pleased Mary too much because the marshal was not of impeccable character. He was cold and plain-speaking, harsh almost, to everyone. Except Nestor. Maybe he saw something in the boy that she didn't, because he seemed to have infinite patience with the young lad.

And now Nestor was a lawman, too. He was full grown, twenty years of age, and had taken the badge as territorial marshal and had proven quite adept at his profession. Now he was God knows where with his best friend Wiley, and she never knew when he would return to visit. Every day as she rose from her bed at dawn her first thoughts were of Nestor; that maybe this day would be the day she would hear his footfall on the porch and his voice calling to her as he came home once more. She kept his small room empty, refusing to rent it out, just in case.

Today, she was hoping he would *not* come home, for Stacy Leech was in town. Stacy Leech was a bad man with a bad name; maybe there was a connection. He was foul-tempered and quick to fight with his fists or his gun. He had killed several men already, nobody seemed to know just how many, and enjoyed prodding smaller and weaker men until they were forced to take the humiliation of flight-or-fight. If there had been any justice in the world, Leech should have lost some of those fights, but he always seemed to win, often beating his opponent long after the fight had gone out of him.

He and Nestor had gone at it frequently as they were

growing up, and Mary had no doubt that should the opportunity present itself, Leech would take on Nestor again, and she was afraid of the outcome. It was different when two boys were whaling away on each other. Now they were young men, and maybe one of them would end up seriously injured or even dead. And so she hoped Nestor would stay away until Leech finished up what he was here for and left town.

"Mrs. Allen, the biscuits are done," Martha said, startling Mary out of her reverie. Mary looked at the untouched cup of tea on the table before her. Land sakes, she was turning into a real slugabed, sitting and remembering instead of working. She rose, wiped her hands on her apron and went to check on the meat. Martha was already checking the meat by the time Mary got there.

"Looks fine," Martha said, and Mary nodded and studied the young girl. Just turned sixteen she was, but she had not yet turned into a full woman, although it was easy to see she would be a beauty in just another year or so.

Mary liked Martha, liked her a lot, even though Martha had a habit of sometimes letting her mouth get ahead of her brain. Like the time she had told Mary that she was in love with Nestor, and was going to marry him first chance she got.

"Land sakes, child," Mary had said. "You are not yet full grown. How can you possibly know that Nestor is the man to make you happy?"

"My mind is full grown," Martha had told her. "I just have to wait for my plumbing to catch up."

Mary had been shocked and told her so too, but later in her room she got to thinking on it and laughed out loud all by herself. She went to sleep smiling about it, and woke up with the same smile on her face. Land sakes, what a girl!

"Somebody at the door, Mrs. Allen," Martha called, and Mary went out to see who it was. Stacy Leech stood there, big enough to fill the door frame, hat in hand.

"Howdy, Mrs. Allen," he said, a little nervous. "I was told you have a room available and I would like to rent it for a month or so, if it's all right with you."

"Hello, Stacy," she came back, seriously. She did have the drummer's room empty now, and she could always use some extra money. Stacy was trouble 'most everywhere he went, but maybe he would take care not to foul his own nest, so to speak. She opened the door.

"C'mon in," she said. "I'll show you the room, and we'd be happy to have you stay with us." He looked a little surprised, obviously not expecting to be welcomed so openly and clearly uncomfortable with the idea that he was not feared.

"Thank you, ma'am," he said meekly, and he followed her upstairs.

Later, while she was getting ready to serve dinner, she got to thinking on him. It seemed strange that a man like Stacy would take a room like he did. He was a drifter, always had been, and for him to settle long enough to rent a room for a full month should tell her something, but for the life of her she couldn't figure out what. He hadn't said, either, and Mary wondered what the big man wanted in this area. It probably boded no good for someone, however, and she hoped Nestor would stay gone for just a little longer.

She sat at the head of the table, of course, with the quiet Mr. Walters and his wife on her left. Stacy sat like some kind of monument at the other end of the table and the new clerk at Patterson's General Store, Mr. Wicker, sat next to him. Martha's chair was next to his. At her special rate of six dollars a week, she could look forward to the grand sum of eighteen dollars a week, not a sum to be trifled with. Of course, once she purchased food (mostly meat since she grew her own vegetables), that cut down on the sum considerably, but all in all, she had enough to be comfortable. As long as she kept taking in boarders, that is.

Martha came in from the kitchen with the roast on a platter surrounded by small potatoes and carrots. She set it in front of Mary to carve, and on an impulse, Mary told her to take it down to Mr. Leech for that purpose.

"Ladies and gentlemen," she said. "We have a new boarder, an old acquaintance of my family, Mr.

Stacy Leech.'' Mr. and Mrs. Walters murmured their hellos and Mr. Wicker nodded at the newcomer.

Stacy appeared flustered as Martha sat the platter in front of him, but he took the carving knife in one hand, fork in the other and began to carve the roast in thick man-sized slabs. He proceeded to fill his plate with enormous amounts of everything, then passed the platter on to Mr. Wicker. Martha returned from the kitchen with the bread still warm from the oven, and gave that to Stacy, who cut a large slab, fully a quarter of the loaf. Mary smiled into her hand. She did like to see a real man eat. Nestor, too, ate like that.

''You going to be with us long, Mr. Leech?'' This came from Mr. Wicker. Stacy looked up from his plate, took in Mr. Wicker with a glance, and returned to his eating.

''Don't know,'' he said.

''Business or pleasure?'' Mr. Wicker went on.

Stacy looked at him again like a man might study a bug. ''Yes,'' he said.

Mr. Wicker finally took the hint and returned to his eating.

''Delicious, as usual, Mrs. Allen,'' said Mrs. Walters. Her husband mumbled his appreciation through a mouthful, and Mr. Wicker also expressed his pleasure.

''Martha did most of the work,'' Mary demurred. Martha smiled.

''How do you like it, Mr. Leech?'' she asked. Stacy

raised his eyes to Martha and suddenly Mary knew why he was here.

"Just fine, ma'am," he mumbled. "Best I ever ate."

Well, well, well. So that was it. Stacy had a thing for Martha. Guess maybe she was more full-grown than Mary had thought. Bound to get more interesting around the place for a while anyway.

"You figure they're gone?" Wiley asked. Nest studied on the prairie.

"Seems like it to me," he allowed.

"You want me to go out and see?" Rebecca asked, and Wiley snorted a laugh. Nest looked over at her, somewhat annoyed.

"That's just what we want," he said sarcastically. "We need a young girl to go out and be sure it is safe for two grown men." She studied him coolly.

"You seem pretty touchy about it," she said. "I was out there once, you remember. I believe you were here lying on your belly at the time." Nest's face reddened with anger, not made any better by the sound of Wiley cackling his silly laugh. Nest glared over at his friend. Wiley stopped laughing, but a grin split his face from ear to ear.

"I think we ought to let her go," he said. "Serve them Indians right." In spite of himself, Nest had to smile back.

"I believe I can handle it," he said. "I'll let you

know if I need any help, though.'' Rebecca took him seriously.

"As you wish," she said.

Nest thumbed back the hammer on his Winchester and took out of the swale, running hunched over. Wiley was covering his friend with his rifle, hoping he wouldn't have to use it again. In about five minutes, Nest came walking back casually.

"It's okay," he said. "You can come on out." They got to their feet and brushed the dust from their clothes.

"I found where there were four of them lying out there," Nest went on. "Less than a hundred yards away. Found another spot where one of them had been hit hard. Must've figured their medicine was bad or something and pulled out."

Wiley laughed. "Prob'ly saw that Rebecca was with us and figured they didn't have a chance," he said as he led their horses out of the swale. "You'd better take her with you," he went on. "I took a stone out of Buck's hoof earlier this morning and he is a little tender-footed."

Nest mounted, swung his leg forward, and motioned Rebecca to the empty stirrup. She swung up behind him and Rusty sidestepped a few times getting accustomed to the new weight. She moved around some, adjusting her skirt to retain a modicum of modesty, then put her arms around his waist.

"I am ready, Mr. Nest," she said.

"Just Nest," he said. "Short for Nestor."

"Surely you have a family name," she said. Her arms were warm around him and she didn't feel nearly so much like a child where she was pressed up against him.

"Allen," he said. "Nestor Allen."

"Very well, Mr. Allen," she said. "I am ready." He touched Rusty with his heels and they started out, backtracking toward her wagon and its dead.

Yellow Knife looked down on his friend, Three Fingers. He had dirt and grass in his hair from them dragging him across the prairie, but at least he would get the proper ceremony for the dead. His eyes were half-open and he was no longer a man but just a man's shell; his home from which he had gone. No living man could emulate that expression and posture.

Yellow Knife was really looking at the wound, the small puncture hole in Three Finger's upper chest. In his mind he could see the horrible blasted-out maw of the exit wound in his back. The raw power of just a single shot, the massive damage done by the white man who casually reached out and struck down Three Fingers from such a far distance, shocked Yellow Knife. And changed him, too.

The joyous anticipation of battle he had felt as a boy was replaced with something else, and it was something he was not certain he liked. It was not good for a warrior to be too cautious. Caution could be mistaken for fear, and men in his tribe would rather die than be thought something less than mighty warriors. The humiliation of such a reputation would be more than any self-respecting warrior could bear. His reputation was already going to take a hit because of the incident with the white girl. On the other hand, he was less than anxious to be the owner of an awful wound like Three Fingers.

"You take Three Fingers home," he said. "I am going to follow the white men for a while." Crooked Fist looked at him.

"Why?" he asked. "What do you want to do?"

"I would like to learn about them," Yellow Knife responded. "Perhaps they will get careless and I can get one of their long guns . . . or maybe even their hair." Actually he had no intention of trying to harm them. What they could do to Three Fingers, they could easily do to him. No. Just following them for a few days would give his reputation a boost, especially if they happened to do something of real interest. Besides, it would be his first chance to see white men and the way they lived.

"Your bow is weak compared to their long guns," Crooked Fist warned. Yellow Knife looked at him with what he hoped was a warrior's expression.

"I am not afraid of their long guns," he said. Crooked Fist looked at him long and hard.

"I am," he said. "And if you wish to return to your home once more, you had better be afraid of them also.'' He turned away and Yellow Knife knew he had been dismissed. He loaded up with food, swung up on his horse, and stepped away from his friends into the emptiness of the prairie.

It was easy to pick up the white men's trail, and he hurried along the tracks, not worried about being seen because the sun was behind him.

Nest patted the earth smooth with the shovel, making it a neat mound that he knew would vanish with the next rain. He straightened and wiped his brow with his shirt sleeve, studying the horizon without thinking about it, for that was the way a man stayed alive out here. Over by the wagon, Wiley and Rebecca were finishing up with cooking, and it would be a good-sized meal on account of they had all the provisions from Rebecca's family wagon to pick from. They would have to leave everything behind when they headed for town.

Nest had said a few words over her folks, and Rebecca had watched without speaking as he and Wiley lowered them into the holes. She had thrown a handful of rich dark earth on each of them, then turned away while Nest covered them up. She had gone a little misty-eyed but had not cried, and Nest had to admit she was some tough girl, and would no doubt grow into some kind of woman.

''Time to eat,'' she called from the wagon, and Nest

picked up his rifle and carried the shovel back to the wagon.

Rebecca had drawn some water from the barrel and set the pitcher and basin on a small table with a towel folded neatly over a bar on one side. She and Wiley had already washed up and were finishing putting the food on the table, so Nest leaned his rifle against the table and proceeded to do the same.

"Hurry up," Rebecca called, "before it gets cold." He wiped his hands quickly, and headed for the table. There was a big hollow just above his belt he was aiming to fill.

Dinner was thick slices of bacon, fried just shy of being crisp, buried under a mound of beans oozing brown sugar and molasses. A separate plate loaded with biscuits finished the meal. There were glasses filled with water at each place on the table, and for an instant Nest thought of home and his Mom. He broke open a steaming biscuit, picked up his fork, and dug in, not holding back at all. Digging graves sure worked up an appetite.

Afterwards, Rebecca brought around the coffeepot and poured their cups full. Real china cups they were, and they certainly looked small in his big hand, but the coffee was delicious. Nest was on his second cup, leaning back in the chair, stomach full and contented before the talk began. He knew there would be talk on account of there was always talk after a meal at a table.

"We have to leave everything here, don't we?" Rebecca asked.

"We do," Wiley said. "We can send someone out from the next town with a team, and they can bring it back for you."

"That's good," she said, but she didn't seem real concerned about it. "How long will it take us to catch them, do you think?"

"There is no 'us' about it," Nest said firmly. "Once we get you safe, Wiley and I will get on after those evil men." Rebecca looked at him hard, and Nest could see the thin veneer on her temper.

"If you take me back to town, it will take us two full days of travel to get there, and two more days for you to get back here again. By then your horse will be worn out and they'll have at least five days' start on you. You will never catch them."

"That is true enough," Wiley agreed. He sipped at his coffee from the dainty little cup. "Seems as though the bad guys are headed in a southerly direction," he went on. "Maybe planning on stopping in Fleet." He sighed. "Reckon we ought to take her with us," he went on. "We can drop her in Fleet when we get there." Nest thought about it for a while. He didn't like the idea of taking a young girl along with them because he didn't know how safe it would be. 'Course she would be just as safe with them as with anyone else, he figured.

"I guess you are right," he said. "She'll be safe

with us and if we do go through Fleet, I can drop her with Mom. I know she'll be well taken care of there.''

Rebecca started doing the dishes while Nest and Wiley talked around the table. All in all it was a pretty homey scene, she thought. A woman taking care of her men.

She studied the two of them as they sat there talking. Wiley was short and stocky. Powerful, was the first word that came to mind. He laughed easily and often, and his laughter was infectious, impossible to listen to without smiling. His face was rugged for such a young man, all crags and deep wrinkles from a lifetime spent out in the weather.

Nestor was tall and slim, by far the more brooding of the two. It was obvious that he was the leader, although the two of them probably didn't realize that fact. It was just a natural occurrence for them, like sun and rain. Nest was the leader and that was that. They doubtless never even pondered on it at all. Her mom had told her that women were always attracted to leaders, and she had to admit she was no exception to the rule.

Of the two, she favored Nest with his quiet ways and controlled attitude. He was a hard worker and would make a good provider. And besides, there wasn't an inch of fat on him anywhere. Lean and strong.

Rebecca shook her head, angry at herself. Shame on her. Her parents were lying over there, not yet buried a full day, and she was thinking about men. She finished up the dishes and carried the dishpan behind the wagon to dump it out. She tossed the contents into the dusk.

Yellow Knife recoiled in surprise as the mass of cool water drenched him from head to toe where he lay. Thinking he had been discovered, he leaped to his feet, raised his arms high, fists clenched at the girl/woman, and gave his fiercest war cry.

"AIIIEEEAAA!!" he yelled.

The dishpan went straight up in the air and Rebecca's yell of shock and fear was just as loud as Yellow Knife's had been. For an instant, time stood still and they looked each other right in the eye. Rebecca's expression was one of wide-eyed open-mouthed shock, and in spite of his own fear, Yellow Knife had to bark a laugh before his wits returned and he took off running silently.

Fear gave wings to his feet, and he ran toward the washstand, grabbed the rifle leaning against it, and took off into the prairie dusk. He heard the two men's chairs fall over as they jumped to their feet and rushed around to see what had caused all the noise. He grinned as he ran, remembering the expression on her face. The stock of the stolen rifle felt silky smooth and slightly warm as he held it in his fist.

He ran for quite a while, then lay in the grass to see if there were any signs of pursuit. He kept feeling the rifle as he lay there, unable to quite believe he had

actually done it, actually stolen the white man's long
gun and escaped with his life. Only problem was that
he had been forced to run in the opposite direction
from his horse. He made up his mind he would lie
where he was until the moon was half across the sky,
then make his way around the wagon and over to his
horse. They would be impressed when he got back to
the village. Even Twisted Hair, the girl who haunted
his dreams, would be impressed. He would truly be
considered a warrior. A white man's rifle!

Nest stared over his pistol sights into the growing
darkness. To say he was confused would be putting it
mildly. Everything had happened too fast, and he had
not yet put together in his mind just what was going
on.

Wiley had been right beside him as they rounded
the wagon, and he had just had time to see Rebecca
pointing into the darkness when he heard a hollow
metallic thump and suddenly Wiley was no longer
there. Nest looked back and Wiley was on the ground,
but from his cursing, Nest could tell he was still alive.
He turned his attention back to the direction Rebecca
had indicated, but could hear or see nothing.

He heard Rebecca moving toward Wiley to help
him.

"I'm so sorry," she said, "but that Indian scared
me near to death!"

Indian! Nest strained his eyes into the darkness, but
it was to no avail. He could see nothing.

"What happened?" he heard Wiley ask. "What hit me?"

"I threw out the dishwater right on top of the Indian," Rebecca explained. "I didn't know he was there or I wouldn't have done it. Anyway, when I got all excited, I threw the dishpan up in the air. I didn't think about it or anything," she went on quickly. "I mean, he jumped up right in front of me and gave out with that awful yell, and the dishpan sort of went up in the air. And it stayed there too, until you ran under it."

"You hit me in the head with the dishpan?" Wiley asked.

"I'm sorry." She was ashamed.

"Look! I'm bleeding."

"It's just a little cut," she explained. Nest smiled into the darkness, then his face split in a wide grin that showed his white teeth, and finally he began to laugh. He laughed hard and he laughed loud.

"I'll tell you something, Nest," Wiley said in a hurt voice. "You have a mean streak in you."

Nest only laughed harder, and in a second Rebecca joined in. The sound of their laughter rolled out into the dark prairie.

Chapter Three

Dishes done, Martha went out to the front porch. It was always her favorite time of day. The work was mostly done, the sun was setting, and it was finally cooling off. She loved to sit in the swing and watch night happen all around her. Sometimes, if some of the other boarders were out there, she would listen to their conversation, but mostly she preferred to have a little quiet time for herself. Today, however, the swing was already occupied. Stacy Leech was sitting there swinging gently.

"Evening," he said.

"Hello, Mr. Leech," Martha replied. She went over and leaned on the pillar by the stairs. She could hear the gentle creaking of the swing; could feel his eyes on her. The door squeaked open and Mr. Wicker came out. He too had started coming out on the porch after dinner every night since he moved in.

"Evening, folks," he said. Then, "Looks like someone beat you to your seat, Martha." She heard the swinging stop instantly.

"Sorry, ma'am," Stacy said. The swing creaked as his weight lifted from it. "Please come and sit," he said. Martha smiled at him.

"Why, thank you, Mr. Leech," she said, and she went over and sat down. It had been a long day and sitting down felt pretty good.

"Kinda thoughtless of me," Stacy said as he sat on the railing. "Just that we used to have a swing like that and it sorta reminded me of home."

"Where was home, Mr. Leech?" Martha asked. It seemed like the polite thing to do.

"First home was in Ohio, ma'am," he said. "Small farm in Ohio."

"You plan on going back there to visit some day?" she asked, surprised to find out she really was interested.

"Not there anymore, ma'am," he said. He hesitated, then added, "Nobody there to go home to, either."

"My family has all passed too, Mr. Leech," Martha said.

"Sorry," he said, and she could tell he meant it.

"My home is in Chicago," said Mr. Wicker. Neither replied. "My sister is still living there, taking care of Mother until I get back.'' Silence. ''Three bed-rooms,'' he went on. ''Two upstairs. Two-story house, don't you know.''

''It must be nice to have a family waiting for you,'' Martha finally said.

''It's a comfort, I tell you,'' he answered. Silence fell on the group once more.

The sun eased below the horizon, painting the western sky a bright red that slowly faded dimmer and dimmer until two small wisps of pink cloud were the only thing visible hanging against the deepening velvet of night.

''Mighty pretty,'' said Leech. Martha assumed he was talking about the sunset.

''Yes it was,'' she agreed.

''Didn't mean the sunset,'' he straightened her out. Martha was shocked. She had no idea how to take his remark; what to do about it. He had just told her that she was pretty! He was a full-grown man and he found her to be pretty! The idea amazed her. Mr. Wicker cleared his throat nervously. The door squeaked open and Mary came out to join them. She hoped it didn't look like she had been standing just inside the door listening, which she had.

''Oh, mercy,'' she said. ''I've gone and missed the sunset again.''

''It was a fine one,'' said Stacy. ''Real . . . pretty.'' Martha felt herself flush in the darkness at the sound of that word coming out of his mouth again. Mary sat down on the swing next to Martha. The sound of crickets floated across the still night.

"This is my favorite time of the day," Mary went on. She looked up at Leech, still sitting on the rail.

"You have been gone from town for quite a while, Mister Leech."

"Yes'm," he replied.

"How long, exactly?" Mary went on. She knew he didn't want to talk about himself, but felt she should find out more about him, especially if he was planning on courting Martha.

"Quite a while," he said.

"About three years, wasn't it?" Mary persisted. He sighed.

"Yes'm," he said. "Three and a half years, near about."

"Was it as nice as Kansas?" she asked.

"Was what as nice as Kansas, ma'am?" he asked.

"Where you were," she explained. "Was where you were as nice as Kansas?" Mary could see his silhouette; could see his gaze switch from her to Martha. He looked at the young girl for a long moment.

"No, ma'am," he finally said. "It surely wasn't." The porch fell silent for a while.

"Being gone so long, Mr. Leech, you probably haven't heard about Nestor," Mary said.

"No, ma'am," he said. He didn't really sound interested.

"He's a federal marshal," Mary said proudly. Suddenly she had his full attention once more.

"He is?"

"Yes." She saw his teeth in the dark as he grinned.

"Well, isn't that something," he said. "Good old Nest is the law." He thought about that for a while. "He expected home soon?" he asked.

"Can't say," from Mary.

"That'd sure be interesting," he said. Mary wasn't sure she liked the way he said that.

"It would?" she asked.

"Yes, ma'am," he said. "It surely would." He got up and the door squeaked as he pulled it open.

"Good night, Mrs. Allen, Mr. Wicker," he said. They echoed the required pleasantries. The door banged closed behind him, then squeaked open once more. "Good night, Martha," he said. "I enjoyed talking to you."

" 'Night, Mr. Leech," she said. "I did, too." The door banged behind him and they could hear his tread as he went up the stairs to his room.

"You know him from before," Martha said to Mary. It was a statement, not a question.

"Yes."

"Seems like a nice fellow," said Mr. Wicker.

"Seems like," Mary agreed. She let the silence build and pretty soon Mr. Wicker began to fidget. He finally got up from the railing.

"Guess I'll turn in, too," he said. He went through

the door and they heard him go up the stairs. The third one from the bottom creaked. It always creaked. The two women sat in silence for a few minutes.

''I wonder what he meant by that?'' Martha finally asked. Mary knew she was talking about Leech and his comment about how interesting it would be if Nestor came home.

''I wonder, too,'' she said.

Yellow Knife was tired. It had been a long, exciting day, what with the fighting earlier and the confrontation with the woman. He was deep, bone-weary tired, but he plodded on through the velvet of the night. The stolen rifle hung heavy in his hand, but it would be the proof of his manhood, his key to respect from his tribe. He knew he had never had anything as fine as that wonderful rifle.

His horse was waiting just a short distance away now, and he had learned a good lesson for a warrior to know. Always leave the horse where he could run straight to it, instead of on the other side of the enemy camp. Even the women would laugh if they could see him now, walking miles that he wouldn't have had to walk had he but thought it through before he rushed in. The thirst for adventure had clouded his judgment, drawing him ever nearer to the white man's camp. He would take time to reason next time.

He had watched them dig the holes and bury their dead, and he had wondered how the dead had died.

When night fell heavy on the prairie he had crawled closer, taking cover behind the wagon. He had been able to hear their voices, listen to the strange inflections of their language; been able to hear them laugh, even. He found it strange that white men and women could laugh just like the Sioux did. Somehow it made them seem more human, more deserving of study. Where there was laughter, maybe there could be understanding and tolerance. The stars shone hard and bright in the sky and the sliver of moon gave just enough light that he could see where he was going.

He came upon his horse almost as a surprise and realized he had practically been asleep as he walked. He would ride a few miles, then rest. With great effort he swung up on the horse, grabbed the reins and booted the animal with his heels. The horse did not move. Yellow Knife kicked him again, and the horse stepped a few tiny steps forward, then stopped once more. The horse was lame. Just what a warrior needed.

He swung down, laid the rifle in the grass and slid his hand down the horse's front legs. Just above the hoof he found a leather thong wrapped around the leg. The thong led over to the other leg and it was tied there. He pondered on that for an instant. It took him a little longer than it should have because he was very tired; then he realized what was going on. When he straightened, he could easily see the white man standing there pointing his pistol right at his heart. Yellow

Knife heard footsteps behind, as another man came up on him.

"Just hold still and don't do anything foolish," Wiley said from behind his gun. Yellow Knife didn't understand the words, but he got the meaning. A frantic need to escape surged through him, a need to fight and die if need be, like the warrior he so desperately wanted to be. Thoughts of Three Fingers and his awful wound entered his mind and poisoned his spirit. Shame flooded through him as he felt the man behind put a leather thong around his hands and tie them together behind his back.

One man took up his horse while the other tied a rope around Yellow Knife's neck, and the three of them started walking across the prairie toward the wagon, one man leading the horse, the other leading Yellow Knife. Shame burned hot in Yellow Knife. Why had he not fought? Fought like a cornered animal, which is what he was. Why had he not died like a man, to be welcomed into the next world by his warrior ancestors, instead of submitting to the fear of the white man's gun like some frightened child? They would probably kill him anyway. He licked his lips with his dry tongue. Even though it wasn't very warrior-like, he hoped they would at least give him a drink of water before they killed him.

They could smell the fire long before they could see the glow of it in the distance, and they walked on across the prairie. It would be dawn in a few more hours.

The fire had burned down to embers and there was nobody around the camp when they wearily walked in. Wiley threw several pieces of wood on the fire, then added a couple of buffalo chips, and soon the fire was casting a circle of red light around the camp and off the sides of the wagon. Yellow Knife stood tall and straight in the center of the camp and watched as the woman climbed out of the wagon where she had been awaiting the men's return.

Nest led Yellow Knife to the wagon, pushed him down by the wheel and tied his hands through the spokes. The woman came up and looked at Yellow Knife.

"That's the one," Rebecca said. She looked at the Indian, who stared back impassively. "He's awful young," she added. "Little more than a boy, really."

"He looked pretty big when he was behind the wagon, didn't he?" Wiley asked. He was smiling. Rebecca laughed.

"Big as a house and twice as mean," she said. She studied the young warrior. "Bet he'd like a drink," she said. "Must get pretty thirsty what with all that stealing and pillaging."

"So give him a drink," said Nest. He was spreading his bedroll out by the fire.

Rebecca took a scoop of water from the barrel and held it up to Yellow Knife's lips. The boy/man stared at her for a moment, then drank greedily from the ladle. She gave him another and another before he was satisfied.

"Probably hungry, too," she said. Nest looked over at her, annoyed.

"Well, he can wait till morning like the rest of us," he said. He pulled off his boots, took his pistol to hand, and crawled into the bedroll. "Good night," he said, and promptly fell asleep. Wiley spread his roll across from the fire and was also asleep in just a few minutes.

Rebecca looked at the young Indian, who looked back. She wondered what the two men were going to do with him in the morning.

"Good night, Indian," she said. The boy/man held her eyes for a moment, then gave a slight nod that surprised her. She was still thinking about it when she crawled back into the secret room in the wagon and fell asleep.

Thirty-five miles to the west was another camp, coals wavering heat into the night sky. The huddled forms of four men sprawled in their bedrolls lay scattered around the fire like tossed-out garbage. The fifth man was a little distance away, wearily looking into the dark, careful not to look into the camp so the firelight would not destroy his night vision. Besides, he was tired of looking at those other four miserable excuses for humanity.

Jubil Wash rubbed his tired eyes and looked into the dark. Far as he could tell, there wasn't a thing out there. Crickets were sounding loud and clear from all points of the compass, and they were a never-miss indicator of movement. If they got quiet all of a sudden, he would snap alert. Otherwise he was lost in thought; living in memory, for life was much better there.

Beth was still alive in his memory; still alive and warm and laughing as she waited for the birth of their first child. She'd had a lovely smile, white teeth straight and clean. He had loved her more than life itself, and would have cheerfully traded places with her even now, so that she could still be alive. For the earth seemed poorer for her passing. And so did he.

His honor was gone. So important when she was alive, it didn't seem worth thinking about now that she was gone. It was easier to stay alive if he stole, so he did. It was easier to stay alive if he cheated and lied, so he did. It was easier to stay alive if he killed without thought, so he did. Staying alive was all that mattered anymore, although for the life of him he couldn't say why.

The men he was with were indicative of his state of mind. Truly the scum of the earth. Failures in everything they ever tried. Failures even as human beings, they managed to stay alive by stealing the results of other men's labor . . . or women's labor if they had a mind to. Jubil had seen them steal everything from livestock to pies cooling on a window ledge, and those less-than-men creatures gave no more thought to it than they did to breathing.

Of the four, he disliked Reb the least. At least Reb was quiet. He never spoke much, and Jubil thought Reb probably didn't like any of his companions any more than Jubil did. Jubil had often thought of the two of them just leaving the other three, only it was just easier to go on the way they were. Besides, sometimes having men with no honor or principles around came in handy. Far as he knew, there was nothing those three wouldn't do if he told them it should be done.

'Course they did get out of hand every now and again, like when Amos killed those two at the wagon. It was hard to understand a man who would rather kill than not kill. He had ended the life of two innocent people that very morning, and he was over there snoring softly, totally unperturbed by the ramifications of his action.

Jubil shook his head into the night. It was a strange way for a teacher to wind up, and that was a fact.

"Pretty quiet tonight," Reb said softly into his ear. In spite of himself, Jubil jumped.

"Good Lord!" he said. "You like to scared me to death!" He could see the flash of Reb's teeth as he grinned.

"Sorry," Reb said. He didn't sound the least bit sorry. They sat in silence for a few minutes.

"You couldn't sleep?" asked Jubil, finally.

"Naw. Kept thinkin' on that couple Amos killed. Don't seem right, somehow. Man and wife live all those years through thick and thin, out tryin' for their dream. Only it all comes to an end on account of some useless, bitter, twisted old man. All them years of living wasted; wasted for thirty-two dollars and four horses." Jubil couldn't remember the last time he ever heard Reb talk so much. He thought for a while.

"Life is hard," he finally said.

"Dyin' ain't," Reb said, back to his clipped speech. "You can turn in," he finished. Jubil cradled his rifle in his arm and rose to his feet. His knees hurt. Getting older. He turned toward the fire.

"Sometimes I think maybe the world would be better off without them three," Reb said to his back. Jubil stopped.

"Maybe better off without any of us," he said, then headed for the camp.

Rebecca woke first. She figured it was her job to see to the men, just like her mom would have done were she not out there lying under the sod. It was too soon for her to really start missing her folks, and in a way she thought it was kind of romantic that they died as they had lived, together. Their graves would soon disappear into the living prairie, but they would be side by side forever.

She tried to be as quiet as she could be, getting out of the wagon, but the Indian was watching her when she came around the corner. He was lying on his side, hands twisted through the spokes of the wheel. It looked pretty painful to Rebecca, and she moved toward him to help him sit upright.

"I wouldn't do that, ma'am," Nest said. "Sometimes they can be like rattlesnakes and strike when you least expect it. Probably be best if you never did touch him at all." He began to roll out of his bedroll.

"I just wanted to help him," she said. "That looks so uncomfortable, he must be suffering." She turned away from the young Indian and went over to the fire. "Sorry I woke you," she added. She began to build up the fire, getting preparations under way for breakfast.

Nest pulled on his boots, then walked over to Yellow Knife. He took him by the shoulders and raised the boy/man to a sitting position that took the strain off his bound hands. Yellow Knife gazed at him impassively, refusing to show the relief he felt inside. Nest looked down on his prisoner.

"You'd like to cook me over a slow fire, wouldn't you, boy?" he said. When he got no reaction, he turned and headed back to the fire. Rebecca already had the coffeepot heating.

Martha always hated going to the general store because she had to walk past the front door of Morty Taylor's Saloon. She could sometimes hear men laughing in there, could smell the odor of liquor, but it was Morty Taylor that made her journey so unpleasant.

He would always come to the door before she got there. He would watch her come with that nasty expression on his face. Sometimes he would say things that were all right on the surface, but his tone left no doubt that he was not thinking the purest of thoughts. She would walk on by without acknowledging him at all, but she could feel his beady little eyes on her every step until she entered Murphy's General Store.

She had tried walking on the other side of the street, but that had proven to be worse because Morty had come right out of his saloon, crossed the street, tipped his hat, and then walked about six steps behind her all the way to Murphy's.

She picked up her basket and sighed. Oh, well. Nothing she could do about it because she had to go to Murphy's almost every day. The boarders had to eat and it was her job to do the shopping. She opened the front door and walked out on the porch.

"Morning, Miss Martha," said Stacy. He was sitting on the railing, and his glance took in her basket. "Heading for Murphy's?" he asked.

"Morning, Mr. Leech," she responded. "Yes, I am. Have to keep feeding your boarders, you know."

"I was figuring on going down there myself," he came back. "Mind if I walk along with you?"

"Sure don't," she said. "Appreciate the company."

He rose and swung into step beside her. She hadn't realized before just how tall he really was.

"How do you like living with Mary Allen?" he asked as they walked. His boots thumped on the boardwalk beside her. Martha looked ahead. She could see Morty's head peering out over the swinging doors, looking for her, most likely.

"Closest thing to a permanent home I've had in a long time," she replied. "Mary treats me like family."

"Must be nice," he came back.

"It is," she said. They walked in silence. Morty had spotted her, and she could easily see his face above the door as he watched her coming down the boardwalk.

" 'Course you won't be living there forever," Stacy said. Martha looked at him. He was avoiding her gaze.

"Whatever do you mean, Mr. Leech?" she asked.

"Well," he went on, "a pretty woman like you must figure on getting married someday and having a home of her own." Martha was becoming interested in the conversation.

"Oh, I suppose so," she replied, casually.

"You, uhhh, have a beau, do you?" he asked, then quickly added, "Ain't none of my business really, so if you don't want to say, that's fine with me." Martha smiled up at him. Now she knew what was going on, and she was amused by his obvious embarrassment. She had never told anybody but Mary about her plan to marry Nestor, so her answer was easy.

"Too busy for that foolishness, Mr. Leech," she said. He looked up and caught her eye for a split second, then looked away again as he pondered on her words.

"I see," he said. They were right at Morty's place, and Morty was hanging over the door, eyes bright, looking past Stacy like he wasn't there.

"Well, hellloo there, beautiful," he said in a nasty tone of voice. Martha pointedly looked away and kept walking. Stacy dropped back a step. There was a meaty sounding thump and Stacy went on as if Morty had never said anything.

"I see how hard you work all the time," he began. Martha glanced back. Morty was gone, the saloon doors swinging slightly. It took her a second to put together what had happened. "Seems like you should be putting all that work toward your own home instead of somebody else's," he finished. She looked up at him again, really seeing him for the first time. He looked back at her, for the first time looking her right in the eye. "Woman needs a man to see to her," he said, "especially out in this country." She held his eyes for a moment, but this time it was Martha who looked away, flustered.

He had obviously taken care of her problem with Morty; taken care of it with a mere swipe of his hand, with no more thought or effort than he would have used to swat a fly. Something that had been such a worrisome thing to her, and he had vanquished it just like that. Besides, he thought she was pretty!

"I am hardly old enough to worry about becoming a homemaker," she said. "I am but sixteen." He laughed softly. It was a nice laugh.

"My mom had been married a year at your age," he pointed out. They were at Murphy's front door. Martha looked up at the big man.

"So had mine, Mr. Leech," she said, and entered the store.

Chapter Four

Yellow Knife was upwind of the fire, but in spite of that he was convinced he could get an occasional whiff of the food cooking over there. His stomach rumbled so loud he thought surely the white people would hear, but they appeared to pay no attention to him. He wondered what they were going to do to him, and he hoped that whatever it was, they would feed him first. At the moment he didn't feel much like a great warrior.

He watched as the big white man, the one they called Nest, came walking over to him. He hoped the fear he felt didn't show in his eyes.

"Relax, young fellow," Nest said. Yellow Knife didn't understand the words, but the tone was soothing. Nest tied his ankles together and Yellow Knife lay there completely helpless. The man called Nest pulled his knife and Yellow Knife narrowed his eyes as he wondered what it was going to feel like to be killed.

Nest was surprised at the hint of fear that showed behind the Indian's eyes. He reached forward and cut the captive's hands free. Rebecca's brought over a plate of food and carefully placed it on the ground where the Indian could reach it. She stuck a spoon in the beans and scooped some water from the barrel into a cup which she put beside the food.

Yellow Knife was amazed. Perhaps the stories he had heard were not true. Perhaps the whites were not savages after all. The two men were at that very moment discussing his fate.

Wiley spoke around a mouthful of beans. "What you plan on doing with him?" Rebecca snapped to attention. She wondered about that, too.

"Figured we'd eat him later," Nest said. "Lots of good meat on Injuns." Rebecca's eyes widened. He sounded serious! Wiley nodded.

"You caught him, you clean him," he said. Nest shook his head.

"You caught him," he pointed out. "Besides, I figured I'd be the one to dispatch him on account of I have seen you shoot." Wiley looked at his friend.

"I can hit him if I am standing right next to him," he said. " 'Specially if you hold him for me." Rebecca finally figured she was being put on.

"If you are going to hold him while Wiley shoots him," she said to Nest, "can I have your horse?" Nest snorted a laugh and Wiley looked disgusted.

"Not you, too," Wiley said to her. She gave him an innocent smile. He shook his head in mock disgust and shoveled another spoonful of food into his mouth.

Yellow Knife belched noisily. He had bean sauce running down his chin and his empty plate was sitting on the ground in front of him. He was looking at Rebecca, eyes bright. Nest smiled.

"Seems like our guest is taken with your cooking," he said to Rebecca. She looked at Yellow Knife and smiled. He looked at her for a few seconds, then the corners of his mouth turned up slightly and he smiled back.

"Well I'll be . . ." said Wiley. "I never saw an Indian smile before. Not ever."

"Me neither," Nest agreed. " 'Course, this is a young one." Rebecca got up from the table, went over, and picked up the Indian's plate. She motioned toward him with it in a gesture that could not be mistaken for anything else. Yellow Knife hesitated, then nodded. The food was the best he had ever eaten. It had a delightful flavor from something he couldn't identify. It was the first time he had ever tasted sugar.

The young woman filled the plate with beans again, laid a couple more strips of bacon on top, and handed it back. The Indian took it from her hand, picked up the unfamiliar spoon, and began to eat noisily. The three watched him eat while they finished up their own breakfast. Rebecca poured them coffee and Wiley leaned back dangerously in the wooden chair, sipping at the hot brew.

"He's liable to be the first fat Indian I ever saw," he observed.

"You aren't going to kill him, are you?" Rebecca asked. Nest made a face.

"Naw," he said. "He's barely more than a boy. I don't have any desire to shoot him, and Wiley there probably couldn't hit him if he wanted to." Wiley looked offended. "I guess we'll just let him go," Nest finished.

"I don't suppose he can bother us any," Wiley said.

"Not unless he brings his friends and relatives back down on us," Nest said. Rebecca sobered. She hadn't thought of that.

"He wouldn't do that, would he?" she asked. Wiley smiled grimly.

"He might," he said. "They have rules in their society just like we do, only they are different rules than the ones we live by. You can never tell what an Indian is going to do next."

"I can't believe he would want to kill us," she said as she looked at Yellow Knife. He was busy wiping the bean sauce from his chin with the back of his hand. He gazed back at her impassively.

Yellow Knife had changed his opinion of the woman now that he had eaten her cooking. She would make a fine wife for a man if only she were not so scrawny and sickly looking. A man might overlook her appearance, though, because she was such a fine cook. She would need training in the ways of the tribe, but a man could grow fat around his fire with her cooking.

He became angry with himself for wasting his remaining time with such idle thoughts. He must figure out how to escape, how to stay alive. But the man who had tied his feet had known what he was doing. There was no way Yellow Knife could slip out of the binding, and he knew what would happen if he tried to untie his legs.

The men put the furniture back in the wagon while the woman cleaned the dishes. She saved the coffeepot and cups for last, and they had one last cup of coffee before Nest put out the fire. They were getting ready to move on, and Yellow Knife knew that whatever life was to bring to him, it would be soon.

He watched as the woman went over to the graves and stood there for a long time with her head bowed. He understood she was praying to her god, praying for the spirits of her parents. He hoped they would not put him under the ground like that after they killed him.

Nest took Rebecca's saddle out of the wagon and put it on the Indian's horse. The horse didn't like it one bit, but Nest had spent all his life with horses, and finally the animal settled down.

"I hate to take a man's horse out here," he said, "only if we leave him afoot, by the time he gets back to his friends we'll be long gone. Seems safest to me."

"Me, too," said Wiley. "It would make me real happy never to see him again or any of his friends either."

Yellow Knife watched as Rebecca rode his horse around the wagon a few times, getting used to the animal and getting the animal used to her. Treacherous beast, the horse soon acted like the woman had been her owner all along. Yellow Knife figured that if he lived, someday he would find that horse and cut its heart out.

Wiley mounted and waited. Nest took Yellow Knife's knife and stuck it in the wooden side of the wagon, then caught up his horse and mounted. He looked down on the Indian, lying there on the ground. Their eyes held for a moment, then Nest nodded slightly. Yellow Knife finally nodded back almost imperceptibly. Wiley booted his horse into motion, Rebecca followed, and Nest brought up the rear.

Yellow Knife watched then single-file away into the prairie. In a minute, he reached down and began to fumble with the knot binding his legs together.

Jubil and Reb were at one end of the beat-up bar, watching the other three down at the other end. Amos was drinking seriously, paying Rafe and Webb no mind as he poured shots and downed them in a businesslike manner. Rafe and Webb were drinking hard too, shots and beers, only they appeared to be having a good time doing it. All three of them seemed bound and determined to drink up their share of the thirty-two dollars they took from the couple they killed on the prairie.

"Bet those folks worked hard and saved long to get that money they are spending so foolish," Reb said. Jubil nodded and sipped at his beer.

"Yup," he replied. "They'd be turning over in their graves to see what their hard work has bought . . . and for whom."

They prob'ly would not think too highly of us, neither," Reb said. Jubil shrugged.

Rafe put down another shot of cheap bar whiskey, picked up his beer, and limped over to the door. Jubil wasn't certain what had happened to Rafe's leg. Probably broken once and not set properly, but it forced the boy to walk with a painful limp. Probably explained his mean streak and dangerous temper, too. Besides, he had the mind of a child. He had the gun of a man, though, and was fast as could be with it when he wanted to be.

"Whooee, Webb," he said as he looked over the top of the swinging doors. "Come lookee here." He was watching a young girl come out of the general store just down the street. There was a man with her, but he paid him no mind. Webb walked over, carrying his beer in his hand.

The two of them looked out at the girl now walking their way. She was engrossed in conversation with the man, apparently oblivious to their presence. Morty watched from behind the bar. He knew what they were looking at. He could warn them about the nasty disposition of the man with the girl, in fact his nose had just quit bleeding, but he didn't. Be kind of nice to see someone else get punched. Rafe stepped through the door and faced the woman.

"Howdy, miss," he said. "How about you c'mon in and have a drink with me. I got lots of money, girl," he added as he gave out his weird laugh.

The couple stopped dead, the man studying Rafe for a moment.

"The lady's with me, boy," he said quietly. Rafe appeared to notice the man for the first time. He looked surprised that anybody would attempt to interfere with him.

In the bar, Jubil shook his head in disgust and got to his feet. He didn't take kindly to a man accosting innocent women in the street, and figured on going and bringing Rafe back inside.

"I can fix that," he heard Rafe say, and a split second later there was a single shot from just outside the door. Jubil brushed Webb to the side and burst through the doors, furious with Rafe. Imagine him shooting down another man for no reason, a man who was just protecting his lady.

Rafe was on the ground flat on his back. He was

breathing in short gasps, and the expression on his face was one of disbelief; of utter shock. A spreading crimson stain smeared his shirt just below his ribs. Fast as he was, his gun was barely half out of his holster. The stranger was standing there, gun already put away, watching Jubil closely.

"Rafe drew first," he heard Webb say from just behind him. Webb was warning him about the stranger; warning him that the man could draw like chain lightning itself. Jubil looked at the girl standing there wide-eyed, then at Rafe lying on the boardwalk.

"Hard way to learn manners," Jubil said. The stranger shrugged. He took the girl by the arm and started to lead her away. She was obviously still shocked by the violence that had happened so close and so incredibly fast.

"There a doctor around here?" Jubil called after them.

"Over the livery," the stranger said over his shoulder, but they didn't stop walking. Jubil looked at Rafe.

"Webb, you and Amos get him over to the doc. I'll be along later."

"I got a sore back," Amos whined. Jubil looked at him hard. "Okay, okay," Amos said. "C'mon, Webb, let's go. My beer's gettin' warm." The two men took Rafe's arms and legs and none too gently hauled him down the street, Rafe sagging between them. Jubil could easily hear Rafe grunting each time they jerked on him. Reb was leaning on the swing doors, looking at him.

"Fair fight?" he asked.

"Fair?" Jubil repeated. "Not hardly. Rafe drew on the guy without warning."

" 'Pears to have been a mistake," Reb observed, then disappeared into the dark interior of the bar.

"Mighty stupid way to die," Jubil agreed. He heard Rafe scream in pain and looked down the street to where the two men had just dropped him and were in the process of picking him up again. Jubil shook his head and followed Reb inside.

Martha was walking in a daze. The gunplay had happened so quickly, so without warning, and she could still see the way the heavy slug had knocked the boy backwards; could still hear the savage grunt as the impact of the bullet forced the air from his lungs. She suddenly realized that Stacy was supporting her, holding her upright with one strong arm around her shoulders. It would have been so shocking had he done it just a few moments earlier, but now she was grateful for the support, grateful for the warmth from another human being.

"He . . . he was going to kill you," she finally said. "For no reason, really. He was going to kill you!" The stunned shock was clear in her voice. She could see other people rushing out to see what the gunfire had been about.

"It's all over now," he said. "I'm really, really sorry you had to see that, but it's all over now. Try to put it out of your mind." She looked up at the big man holding her so gently.

"He was trying to kill you!" she repeated in amazement. Stacy looked down on her face. Her eyes were brimming with tears, and then there was too much moisture there, and the water slid down her smooth cheeks, leaving tiny wet trails. He took his other hand and pulled her head against his chest. Her hair was so soft.

"It's okay, Martha," he said softly. "It's okay." He stood there in the street, holding her close, feeling her body wracked with sobs as she cried against his chest. Over her form he could see Mary Allen hurrying down the street. In a few moments she would be here and Martha would be taken from his arms. He tried to imprint the feel of her in his memory so he could bring it out on some of the long cold nights to come. He wanted to be able to remember the miracle of the moment, the longing he felt to protect her, the wondrous feel of her soft form against his.

Yellow Knife had found a canteen and a butcher knife in the wagon. He had been rather surprised at himself because he went through the wagon carefully without throwing the stuff out to rot after the next rain. It was his way of being nice to the woman who fed him, but it really wasn't the warrior's way and that bothered him some.

He had filled the canteen from the water barrel, stuck the butcher knife in his sheath with his skinning blade and set out to the west. His path almost followed the one the three white people had taken, and he hoped they kept going that way and blundered into the tribe's camp. After a mile or so they curved off to the south, and he realized they were following the tracks of those who had killed the man and woman at the wagon. Vengeance was something he could understand, and in a way he wished them well . . . at least until he caught up with them again.

His feelings toward the whites were all mixed up, definitely not warriorlike. In a way he was insulted. They obviously had not thought him worth killing. On the other hand, that was not altogether a bad thing. They had at least feared him enough that they had kept him bound securely.

They had fed him and given him water so he could stay alive. He did not know why. It could be because hospitality was very important to their race, just as it was to the Sioux. Of course the Sioux did not extend it to their enemies as the three whites had. The greatest honor a Sioux could extend to an enemy was to kill him slowly so he could prove his manhood to his ancestors. That way he would be welcomed as a warrior in the afterworld.

Don Hepler

Yellow Knife pondered on it as he walked hour after hour.

They had taken his horse and that was an irritation and would cause loss of face with the tribe, but he understood that they needed the horse for the woman, and besides, they couldn't take a chance on him getting to his tribe and bringing them back. The fact that he had escaped from them alive would bring honor to him, so in the long run he would probably come out about even.

No. The real loss, the biggest nagging failure of all, was the loss of the rifle. He could almost feel the warm smoothness of it in his hands. Had he been more careful, smarter about where he left his horse, he would be going back to the tribe with great honor instead of walking in with nothing but a butcher knife and a canteen to show for his effort.

He walked on in that steady pace, walked toward the sunset and continued into the darkness. The loss of the rifle, once he had had it in his hands, would not let go of him; would not let him stop or rest. His body had gotten tired the night before, gotten tired and let him down. It would not happen again. He walked into the darkness.

Chapter Five

Yellow Knife had told his story many times, with only small embellishments. It was fantastic enough that he did not need to add anything to it, and he was surprised at how impressed his friends and the elders were with the tale of his adventure. He lay there in the tent of his father, finally allowing his body the rest it had been crying for. The buffalo hides felt soft and warm, and he could hear the women talking outside. He wished his father had lived long enough to hear his story, but supposed the old warrior could see him from wherever he was. His father would have escaped with the rifle, that was certain. Yellow Knife allowed his eyes to close and heard his mother talking outside as she prepared a meal for her lost son. His lips moved just before he slept.

"I will get that long gun," he said to his dead father.

That long gun was riding comfortably in the rifle sheath on the right side of Nest's horse. The night before, he had carefully cleaned it and rubbed it with oil. It was one of the tools of his trade and he took care of it. How often he cleaned it depended on the weather. If it rained, he cleaned it that very night, otherwise it could go for days in dry weather. He had sat next to the fire and cleaned it because the Indian had had it and he didn't know if it had gotten wet or not.

He had been cleaning his rifle, but he had spent a lot of time watching the girl. Rebecca had done the cooking and cleaned up the dishes just like a woman was supposed to do. It was kind of nice to have a woman around the camp, and she could for sure cook better than Wiley.

She had laughed with them and joked with them and never once mentioned her parents buried under the ground but a single day behind them. She was tough; strong as a full-grown woman, but somewhere inside there had to be a pool of grief just waiting to get out. There was certainly a pool of anger in there, and it showed when Nest had told her he was going to leave her with his mom when they got to Fleet.

"It is my intention to accompany you on your hunt until we catch up with those evil men," she said firmly. She was pretty cute when she had that determined expression on her face. Nest sighed.

"Look, Rebecca," he said. "If you were to come along, Wiley would want to make camp early in the day just so he would have more time to eat your cooking. Pretty soon he would get fatter and we would have to slow down just to save his horse. I think it would be best if we went on alone."

"What do you mean, fatter?" Wiley wanted to know, offended. He smacked his hand against his slim, board-hard stomach. "I am not fat," he stated.

"You are feeling in the wrong place," said Nest. "I have been following you all day, and from my angle it looked like you were going to seed, sort of." Wiley looked hurt and Rebecca giggled.

"All of my family were big-boned," Wiley explained, and Rebecca laughed out loud. Again he looked hurt.

"I will go along with the big bone theory," Nest said, "but they appear to be deeply buried from where I sat . . . from where you sat, too." Wiley grinned and patted his hips.

"They're just very well rounded," he explained. The three lapsed into friendly silence for a while. Nest thought he had averted the situation.

"I still intend to accompany you," Rebecca said softly. "If necessary I shall continue alone." Wiley looked at her and smiled.

"Tough little cracker, aren't you?" he asked. She looked at him, dead serious.

"I am a determined little cracker," she said. Nest shook his head.

"I do not wish to hurt your feelings," he said, "but you would slow us down and make it easier for the villains to make good their escape. You do not want them to get away scot-free, do you?" She shook her head.

"Then you must let us do what we do best," Nest said. "We will bring them back to Fleet for trial where you will get a chance to face them and testify against them and probably see them hang later. That should be enough to satisfy even you," he finished.

"I would like to watch them hang," she said. "Especially if you could arrange to have their toes just touch the ground." Wiley appeared taken aback.

"Whoa," he said. "And I thought some men were hard!"

"Women can be hard, too," she said. She didn't look real hard to Nest. She looked pretty soft. No. She looked pretty *and* soft. He leaned back and rubbed on his rifle, wondering where *that* thought had come from.

And now they were riding down toward Fleet. Home. Mom. Good food and a soft bed. And the end of Rebecca being with them. He looked at her back as she rode the Indian's horse just ahead of him.

She was something special, that was certain. Tough

and self-assured. Unafraid. He remembered the first time he had seen her. Was it only two days ago? She had been walking tall and proud across the prairie, her father's big Walker Colt hanging from her hand. She had been really something. She still was really something.

They rode down and turned on the road into Fleet.

Fleet wasn't much of a town. Matter of fact, it only had three streets altogether. There was Main Street, a dusty slash straight through the prairie in the dry season; a motionless river of mud during the rains. There was a side street on either side running parallel to the main street, ending in cross streets that were no more than alleys leading over to the main drag.

Main Street boasted boardwalks, a luxury not yet present on the side streets. Nest's mom lived at the other end of the main drag, one house beyond the end of the boardwalk, which could be an inconvenience, but also gave the place a feeling of still being out in the open country.

The three horses clopped their way down the street, past the general store, past Murphy's Saloon, past Reeve's Gun Shop. Occasionally someone would come to the front of their store to see who was riding through town, but for the most part, nobody seemed to note their passing.

Mary was in the kitchen kneading dough for dinner rolls when the feeling came over her. She straightened from her work and wondered at what she felt. It was like when she was a kid waiting to go to the Saturday dance down at the livery. Something was going to happen. Something exciting. Something wonderful.

"Something wrong?" asked Martha from across the big wooden worktable. Martha was making two pies for dinner; one apple, one from canned peaches.

"No," Mary said. "Everything's fine." She plopped the dough in a large bowl, covered it with a damp cloth and walked through the house to the front door. She walked out to the street, wiping her hands on her apron.

Nothing happening from the west, nothing happening from the east. Wait. Far to the east, out the other side of town, she could see three riders in the distance. She watched. Could it be?

They rode into town and plodded up the dusty street in her direction. Was there something familiar about them? She felt her heart leap. It was. It was her son and his friend. There was a woman riding between them.

So many months he had been gone. So many days she had wondered if he was all right, or if some evil man had hurt her boy, and now all her fears were put to rest. Here he was, looking strong, looking healthy. He was close enough that she could see the flash from his smile as he caught sight of her, and then there they were, swinging down in front of her. Nestor tossed his reins over the hitching rail and held out his arms for her, grin wide and beautiful to see.

"Hi, Mom," he said, and Mary rushed to her boy who was now a man, and tried to hug the stuffing out of him. Nest grinned over her shoulder at Rebecca. Wiley helped Rebecca down, turned, and was immediately engulfed by Mary with the same intensity as her son.

"Howdy, ma'am," he said, sort of embarrassed to have her hugging him in front of Rebecca. After all, he wasn't any kin of hers, just her son's friend. 'Course, she had always greeted him this way too, and he suspected it would be the same even if Nest wasn't along. She could hug pretty hard for an older woman. Actually, he rather liked it. Kind of made him feel like one of the family.

"Mom," Nest said. "This is Rebecca Ward." Mary released Wiley and studied the newcomer. She saw Rebecca as an attractive young woman, and the first time Rebecca looked at her son, Mary felt a twinge of maternal jealousy as she realized this young woman was serious about her boy. Of course Nestor had absolutely no idea of something that Mary found to be so obvious. Men were certainly a little dense when it came to understanding women.

"We found her two days east," Wiley explained. "Her folks were murdered by five evil men." Mary felt her heart go out to the young woman. She could tell that Rebecca was exhausted, not so much by the long hours in the saddle, as by the restrained grief for her parents.

"She will have your room, Nestor," Mary said. "It's the only one available." She turned to Rebecca. "C'mon, honey," she said. "You're as welcome as the sunshine in my home." Rebecca gave her a beautiful smile, and Mary turned to lead the newcomers into the house. There was a sudden squeal from the porch.

"Nestor!" Martha yelled in delight, and she ran down the stairs and threw herself into his arms. Nest was somewhat taken aback to suddenly find a fully developed woman in his arms, but being no fool he quickly swept her into his arms and hugged back just as good as he got.

"My gosh, Martha," he said. "You're all grown up." Mary took note of the sudden stiffness in Rebecca.

"Relax, honey," she said. "They're old friends." Rebecca looked down on Mary.

"Why should I care?" she asked. Mary cackled a laugh.

"Right," she said. "Why should you care," and she laughed again.

Nest couldn't figure why Martha didn't seem too anxious to let go, but he guessed he didn't mind. She felt pretty good pressed against him like that.

"Hey," Wiley finally said. "Don't waste all that big hello on him." Martha let go of Nest and gave Wiley a little hug.

"Hi, Wiley," she said. "It is nice to see you, too."

"Obviously not as nice as it is to see Nest." Wiley affected to pout. Martha laughed and took both men by the elbows and led them toward the house.

Upstairs, Stacy stepped back from the window and allowed the curtains to close. So. Nest was home. And Martha was plainly glad to see him. Stacy sighed and went over to the bed. He lay down, boots and all, to think on the situation. He lay there for a few minutes and began to doze, then snapped awake. He reached up, slid his forty-five out of the holster and held it across his chest, then went to sleep.

Jubil could feel the five-dollar gold piece and the two silver dollars in his pocket, all he had left from the wagon. It was all the money he had in the world.

Didn't seem right that a man his age should still be living hand to mouth like he was. A man his age should have a home and some land; maybe some kids. 'Course he probably would have had all those things if Beth hadn't up and died, but that was just an excuse, really. He sighed. Seven dollars. Not much to show for a man's whole life.

The fact that it was stolen money bothered him too. Been a long time since his conscience had acted up, but guilt was probably the reason that seven dollars felt so heavy in his pocket. It was like even though he had the money in his possession, it still really belonged to the couple Amos had killed. After all, they had *earned* the money, not he. He had just taken it from their dead bodies.

It just didn't seem right to waste it on whiskey, not after they had worked so hard for it, and that was why he still had it weighing heavy in his pocket. Reb must have felt pretty much the same way, because he had only had a couple of beers in Fleet, which meant he still had most of his money too. Amos and Webb were already nearly broke, having spent theirs on strong drink and worse at Murphy's Saloon. Jubil suspected they had also spent Rafe's money after they took it from his wounded body.

Rafe was probably dead by now. Jubil had seen too many wounds, and knew there was no way Rafe could survive after being hit that hard. The stranger must be quite a hand with a gun to put Rafe in his grave so easily. Jubil thought about the young lad for a minute, then shook his head slightly. Nope. Rafe would not be missed. In a week, nobody would know or care that he had ever been alive. It was quite an epitaph for a tombstone: WHO CARES.

That was probably the same way all of them would wind up. Buried in some forsaken little town, to be forgotten by the good people almost immediately. Somehow, Jubil did not think Beth would be very proud of him anymore. She had been once, though. Being married to a teacher had been a source of pride in her. But smart as he was, he could not help her as she lay there and struggled to breathe. He could still remember the weak little smile she gave him, the way her thin hand felt against his face. Then she had just given up like, and died. Right then. While he still felt her hand against him. And then her hand had fallen away, and his life had fallen away. And here he was.

He looked forward at the others. Somehow he could not bring himself to call them his men. Amos was slumped over in the saddle, feeling mighty poor. Webb was sitting tall and stiff as he could be, probably trying not to jar his aching head. Reb, of course, was paying no mind to any of them, riding point and keeping a wary eye to the horizon just like always.

They had pulled out of Fleet last night, heading west from town before swinging around to the north. None of them had asked Jubil where he was taking them; it was like they didn't care. 'Course Amos and Webb really hadn't cared, owing to the condition they were in.

Jubil was heading for Montana. Fresh country. Clean and mostly unspoiled. A man could get a new start up there, and he was ready to do something different. He figured on parting company with the others soon as he figured it was safe to travel alone. He didn't know what they would do without him, and except for Reb, he didn't care much. Maybe he would ask Reb to come along. Reb at least was part of a man.

Jubil couldn't say what it was that snapped him alert. Something, maybe a sound, maybe an odor, jolted into his brain and he was suddenly very, very alert. He saw Reb straighten in his saddle at the same time. It was like they were being watched all of a sudden. He settled himself in the saddle, ready to fight or flee, whichever was required.

They plodded on through the tall prairie grass, sighting nothing, but knowing someone or something was out there watching them. The tension began to build in Jubil. He could *feel* the eyes; *feel* the vulnerability of his back. It was strange. Here he was, a man for whom living held no thrill, yet he was so tense about dying alone and forgotten out here. He thought he heard something off to the right, but could see nothing except the waving of the grass.

Reb rode down into a gully and dismounted. The others followed.

Amos swung down, almost collapsing when his legs met the ground.

"Oh, thank God," he said. "I thought you were going to ride on forever." Reb looked at him with contempt. Webb looked around, finally realizing they had stopped in the middle of the day and there must be a reason.

"What gives?" he asked.

"Don't know," from Reb in his usual laconic style. Jubil could see Webb force his attention outward, ignoring his hangover as he studied the surrounding prairie for danger. Amos took his canteen and plopped down cross-legged in the grass, sucking noisily at his water.

"I'd go easy on that if I were you," Jubil said. Amos just glared at him and swallowed again and again, his scrawny Adam's apple bobbing up and down in his stringy old throat. Jubil shrugged. Amos had been warned. If he ran out of water, that was his problem.

Reb bent over and picked up something from the ground. He held it out for Jubil to see. It was an empty rifle shell. Webb winced as he bent down, head throbbing, and picked up another one.

"Hasn't been here for more than a week, I'd say," from Reb. "Still shiny."

"Somebody had trouble here," Jubil responded.

"Maybe hunting," Webb said.

"Doubt it," from Reb. "Two different calibers. Two rifles. There's a couple more empty hulls over there," he indicated with his head. Webb looked around again, nervous.

"Indians, maybe?" he asked. Reb shrugged in reply.

"Least whoever it was got out of here alive," Jubil observed, almost to himself.

"We should be so lucky," Reb said back, just as soft. "Maybe we should just lay up here for a while. They might not know we are here yet and go right on by."

Out in the prairie a coyote barked sharply. Reb looked at Jubil for a second, then began to unsaddle his horse. Jubil did the same.

"What gives?" from Amos.

"Gonna stay here a while," Jubil said. The coyote that wasn't a coyote barked again. Four hours to nightfall, Jubil figured.

Chapter Six

Rebecca already felt at home. Mary just took her in and treated her like family and in just a few short hours, it seemed like home. In a way, Rebecca felt guilty. It seemed like she should be missing her parents more; grieving instead of setting the table for dinner while she listened to Mary humming in the kitchen. But it was nice after living in that wagon for so long. Nice to be in a real house made of wood. Nice to be in the company of others besides just the three members of her family. Nice to feel safe and secure and not to have to worry about Indians or evil men.

Nest and Wiley had put up the horses in the small barn out back. Then they had cleaned up and sat out on the front porch. She had looked out at them once, and they were just sitting there, not talking much. She supposed they were enjoying the feeling of being back in a real home just like she was. It was the first time she had ever seen them not wearing their gun belts.

Mary rang the chime that announced dinner, and suddenly the house was full of bustling sounds as people made their way to the table. Nest and Wiley sat at the end by Mary, and she happily introduced them to Mr. Walters and his wife, Romona. Mr. Wicker was genuinely glad to see someone new, and the table seemed ever so long with the added board and place settings. The empty chair at the other end of the table piqued Nest's curiosity, but he quickly forgot about it as the food was passed and conversation about their latest adventures got under way.

''So sorry to hear about your parents, dear,'' Mrs. Walters had just said, when conversation stopped as a heavy tread on the stairs announced the pending arrival of the missing guest. Nest was smiling at Rebecca across the table, enjoying her being the center of attention, when Stacy Leech entered the room. Nest turned, a smile frozen on his lips as he recognized his old enemy. Stacy was not wearing a gun.

''Nice to see you, too, Nest,'' Stacy said in response to the frozen smile. He sat down and seemed not to notice the hard look from Nest.

''Sorry I'm late, Mrs. Allen,'' he said. ''Sure smells good.'' Mary watched her son's face harden against her latest boarder. It had always been like that. Oil and water, the two men simply did not mix. There was something there, something she had never been able to find out about, and because of it, her son disliked Stacy Leech more than any other living man. Trying to keep peace between them might be a full-time job for a while, Mary thought.

"It's okay, Mr. Leech," she said. "While we're passing the food I'd like you to meet Miss Rebecca Ward, who was rescued on the prairie by Nestor and Wiley." She turned to Rebecca. "And Rebecca, this is our newest boarder, Mr. Stacy Leech."

At the sound of his name, there was an obvious reaction from Wiley. Stacy looked at him and smiled in a strange way, then glanced at the young woman.

"Howdy, ma'am," he said. "Always a pleasure to meet such an attractive woman." Rebecca smiled at him. She too, had noticed the animosity Nest showed toward this big man.

"Why, thank you, Mr. Leech," she said, and dismissed him completely by looking away.

As the food was passed and eating continued, conversation gradually returned to normal. Nest and Leech did not join in, however. Martha eyed the two men. Maybe she could do something.

"Nestor," she said. "You should be grateful to Mr. Leech. He was my protector yesterday."

"He was?" said Nest. At least she had spurred his interest.

"Yes," she went on. "A nasty young man came

out of Murphy's and attempted to accost me right in the street. Fortunately, Mr. Leech was walking with me at the time.'' She gave a visible shudder. ''He was a horrible young man,'' she remembered, ''with a strange laugh and a limp.'' She didn't notice Rebecca stop chewing and snap to attention as Martha continued.

''When Mr. Leech informed him that he was with me and the young man should go away, the fellow actually began to draw his gun. I have no doubt it was his intention to shoot Mr. Leech dead on the spot.'' She definitely had Nest's attention. In fact, the whole table was silent as she repeated the events that had not been mentioned since yesterday.

''Mr. Leech was forced to take his own pistol and shoot the man down right there in front of me,'' she finished. For a moment, in her mind, she was back there once more. ''I had no idea a bullet could hit a man so hard,'' she said almost to herself. The table was silent for a long moment, and she pulled herself back to the present and saw Nest looking across the table at her, a strange expression on his face.

''I am glad you were not hurt, Martha,'' he said. He looked up at Leech. Their eyes locked for a moment, then Nest nodded slightly. It was obviously difficult for him to acknowledge any kind of debt to Leech. ''Grateful to you,'' Nest said tightly. Stacy allowed a small smile to turn up the corner of his lips, before he returned to his food. Rebecca watched the entire exchange and wondered what was going on that she did not understand. She turned to Martha.

"You said the man had a limp and a strange laugh?" she asked.

"That's right," Martha said. "An awful laugh, like he was not quite right in the head, if you know what I mean."

"Was he alone?" from Rebecca.

"No. He had some friends with him."

"Can you tell me what they looked like, or their names?" Rebecca had everyone's attention now. She was so intense, so serious. Martha shook her head.

"Sorry," she said. "I . . . I wasn't paying too much attention at the time." A look of disappointment flashed across Rebecca's face.

"One was older, maybe forty," Stacy volunteered. "He was the leader, I guess. He had two of the others take the wounded man to the doctor. I believe he called one Amos. I think the one who never came out of the saloon was wearing a Confederate uniform jacket." Martha looked over at Stacy, surprised at how he could remember so much in spite of everything that happened. He was certainly a cool character in a crisis.

"I believe those are the men we are seeking," Rebecca said to Nest. Nest and Wiley looked at each other.

"Are they still in town?" Wiley asked.

"They are gone," said Mr. Wicker. "Heard talk of

them in the store today. Left last night sometime.''
Wiley and Nest relaxed visibly.

''Their dead friend is over in the back room of the
store in a coffin, though,'' Wicker finished.

''He fit to look at?'' Nest asked.

''He shouldn't offend the lady,'' Wicker said. ''I
can take you over there after dinner if you like.''

''I don't like,'' said Nest, ''but we could use an
identification . . . if you are up to it,'' he added to Rebecca. Her expression was hard.

''It would be my pleasure,'' she said, and somehow
her hardness was unsettling. Conversation was pretty
sparse for the rest of Mary's welcome home dinner.

The general store had been around for ten years, and
it had developed a smell of its own, a smell that told
of all the food, all the sweat, all the people that had
passed through on their way to their destiny. It was
not a bad smell, but rather a warm reminder that this
was a building where living happened each and every
day.

The floor creaked under their tread as Nest, Wiley,
Rebecca, and Mr. Wicker walked back past the long
counter to the storeroom. It was getting darker outside,
and somehow being in the closed store seemed a little
bit spooky, especially when Wicker remembered why
they were there.

The door creaked on its hinges when he swung it
open. The boss had asked him to oil it two days ago

already, and that added to his uneasiness. Having the two lawmen along, guns slung on their hips, helped a whole lot, however.

"It's over here," he said, then corrected himself. "I mean, he's over here," and he led them over to the corner. Several rough coffins were leaning against the wall waiting for someone to die. One, however, was sitting across two sawhorses, the lid lying loose on top. Nest and Wiley lifted down the lid and Wicker held the lantern high. Rebecca forced herself to look into the box, to see where this young man was going to spend eternity.

His face was calm, peaceful, and he had the empty look of all dead things. The shell was there, but the living part was gone forever and what had once been a living vital thing was now just a piece of dead meat waiting to be put in the ground away from the sight of mankind forever. It was him, and she couldn't help but wonder, as she looked at what had once been a young man, what had made him turn out the way he had. What could make someone so young become so evil?

"He's one of them," she said with certainty. Nest and Wiley picked up the lid. Rebecca looked on the body, surprised at how little emotion she felt. This man had been part of the group that killed her parents and now he lay dead himself only days later. Mom and Dad were dead, and so was one of their killers, and somehow it seemed not to matter so much. The feeling of satisfied vengeance she had been expecting did not materialize, but rather was replaced with a hollow emptiness. This man's death would not bring her parents back, and she caught her breath as her true loss began to sink in. Wiley and Nest laid the lid on the box and Rebecca stood staring down at it in stunned silence.

Her parents were gone. Never again would she hear Mom call to her. Never again would she hear Dad's voice soften with affection as he talked to her. Never again would she feel surrounded by their warm love. Tears flooded her eyes and slid down her cheeks as the loneliness of forever burned into her.

Nest watched Rebecca cry silent tears for a moment. He had known that nobody could be as hard as she had seemed, and in a way had been expecting that sometime her loss would sink in and overwhelm her. What he hadn't been expecting, however, was the flood of emotion that washed over him as he watched her cry. Without thought he stepped forward and encompassed her with his arms. He felt her heave and twitch against him as she cried into his chest. He looked up into Wiley's confused eyes and tried to hug away some of the pain she was feeling.

"She's sorry he's dead?" Wiley asked softly in a surprised tone. Nest looked at his friend.

"I think she just realized her folks are gone," he murmured, and Wiley nodded in sudden understanding. "Just leave us alone for a few minutes," Nest suggested. "She just needs a shoulder to cry on, I think." Wiley nodded, and he and Wicker went into the store and closed the door softly behind them.

Nest stood there holding her as Rebecca cried into his chest, her muffled sobs tearing at him. He felt her arms go around his back and she held him to her tightly as she let her grief pour into his shirt. He stood there, tall and strong, and felt small and weak as he could do nothing to help her ease her pain, nothing but hold her and let it happen. She felt soft and warm against him, and her arms wrapped around him and held him tight. He put a hand on her hair and held her head against him. Her hair was soft, so soft, and it surprised him because she had seemed so tough before.

In a few minutes, the sobbing slowed and stopped, and still they stood there, the big man and the small woman, locked in each other's arms. Nest could feel the dampness of her tears where they had soaked through his shirt.

"I'm sorry," she said in a small voice, still not letting go or moving. "I don't know what came over me."

"It's okay, Rebecca," he said softly. Her head moved under his hand and she looked up at him. Nest looked down on her, her tear-stained face only inches from his, and he never wanted to kiss a woman more. Her lips were only inches from his, and all he would have to do would be to lean down just a little and touch her lips with his.

But he remembered that she had just been grieving for the horrible loss of her parents, suspected that a kiss would be the furthest thing from her mind, and did not want to offend her with his unwanted attentions. So he stepped back. He moved from her arms, took her by the hand, and led her from the storeroom with its awful case of death, led her back into the front of the store where Wiley and Wicker waited for them.

They walked out of the store and waited in silence while Wicker locked up. The boardwalk sounded hollow under their feet as they stepped off the distance back to the Allen home. Not a word was spoken.

The porch was empty when they arrived, and Rebecca sat in the swing and stared into the darkness. Mr. Wicker figured his presence was not required and retired to the parlor. Wiley and Nest sat on the porch railing, one on each side of the steps, legs dangling. Crickets sounded from the bushes around the house and they listened to the sounds of the night for a few minutes.

"Still four of them to go," Wiley finally said softly.

"Yeah," said Nest. "Probably only a day ahead of us, too."

"Sunup," from Wiley. Nest sighed. So much for his time at home with Mom.

"Sounds about right," he said.

"What about the man we were chasing before?" Wiley asked.

"He will have to wait," Nest said firmly. "These four are far worse, I think."

"Be easy to catch him now," Wiley said.

"Don't fool yourself," Nest cautioned. "Nothing easy about it, I'm thinking." Silence fell for a few more minutes as they each remained buried in their own thoughts. Then Wiley rose and stretched.

"I'm going to turn in," he said. "As I get older, sunup seems to keep getting earlier."

"Good night, Wiley," said Rebecca, and Wiley could hear the affection and friendship in her voice.

"I will see you off in the morning." Her teeth flashed white in the dark.

"Why, that's mighty nice of you," he said, and walked down the steps and proceeded around the back to the bunkroom in the barn. They listened to his footsteps as he went away. Then there was quiet once more.

"I shall see you off too, Nestor," she said. Her tone was soft and silky and Nest couldn't quite grasp what she was trying to say.

"That'd be real nice, Rebecca," he responded. He could see her form as she sat motionless on the swing, feet tucked beneath her. He wanted to go over and sit beside her but he didn't.

"You will be careful," she said.

"Sure," he came back. "Wiley and I are always careful,"

"Catching those men is not worth your life," she went on, as if he hadn't spoken. Nest looked over at her. Was there more there than just friendly concern? He had to find out.

"Rebecca . . ." he began. The door opened and Martha came out.

"Why, here you are," she said. "I was wondering where you were." She plopped down on the swing next to Rebecca.

"Evening, Martha," Nest said, echoed by Rebecca.

"It's a good thing there's no moon," Martha went on, "or I'd be jealous of you two out here alone."

Rebecca studied Martha for a moment, then got to her feet.

"No reason to be jealous," she said. She turned to Nest. "I believe I'll turn in, too," she said. "Good evening, Nestor." Nest wanted to speak to her, wanted to ask her what he needed to know, but the time had passed. Or the time had not yet come.

"Good evening, Rebecca," was all he said, and he watched her go through the door and away from him once more. Martha started swinging back and forth.

"She's very pretty, isn't she?" she asked. Nest studied her.

"Sure is," he agreed. "So are you, though. You have grown into a fine-looking woman while I have been gone," he added.

"Why, thank you, Nestor," she said.

"Must be young men hanging around here all the time, I expect," he said. She laughed.

"Boys call occasionally," she admitted. "But there's not hardly a real man in the whole town." She wondered why he laughed at that.

"And what does it take to make a real man?" he wanted to know. She was easy to talk to, had always been easy to talk to, and Nest didn't have to watch his words or wonder whether she would get his meaning.

"Well he has to be . . . he has to be . . ." and then she giggled as she thought of the right answer. "He has to be like you, Nest." Nest laughed out loud.

"You shouldn't have any trouble finding a man then," he said. "There's lots of them out there who are better than me." The door opened and Stacy Leech came out. The grin disappeared from Nest's face.

"Evening, Mr. Leech," Martha said, and patted the seat beside her. "Why don't you sit down right here. A girl never knows when she's going to need a protector."

"I'd be proud to join you, Martha," Leech said, and proceeded to follow words with action. In a minute they were swinging gently side by side. Martha hoped Nest was getting just a little bit jealous. Nest had grown quiet, and she thought maybe she was right.

"That man I killed one of the bad guys?" Stacy asked.

"Yup," said Nest. "Too bad the others got away."

Stacy said nothing, just enjoyed the closeness of Martha. The silence stretched out as minutes ticked by. More and more crickets added their sound to the night and finally, in spite of herself, Martha yawned.

"Oh, excuse me," she said. "I guess I should be going to bed." Neither man said anything. She rose. " 'Night, Mr. Leech. 'Night, Nestor," she said, wondering what had happened to the happy mood from before. The two men wished her a good night, and she reluctantly went into the house. She was hoping one of them would ask her to stay longer, but it was not to be.

Nest and Stacy listened to her footsteps fade. Nest finally broke the silence.

"Thank you for taking care of her," he said in a flat tone.

"My pleasure," said Stacy. The silence drew out once more.

"Wiley and I are leaving at sunup," Nest said. "We will track down the killers of Rebecca's parents."

"Good," said Stacy. "Awful thing to have happen." Nest rose to his feet.

"You had best be gone before we are," he said, voice calm but hard. The other man thought about that for a moment.

"Am I supposed to be grateful?" Stacy asked.

"That'd be a mistake," Nest said. He hesitated, then went on. "It was a low thing to do, coming to my home like you did. You thought I would not take you here. You were wrong. You saved Martha when she needed saving and I am grateful, but that would not make me forsake my oath. You have fallen to second place on my list because of the death of Rebecca's folks. That means you have a little time to run. Take it. If you are here in the morning I shall take you in or kill you.'' Stacy casually got to his feet.

''I do not kill so easily,'' he said calmly. He headed for the door. ''I shall be seeing you, Nest.''

''You can count on it,'' Nest answered.

Chapter Seven

Nest pushed back from the table.

"Good grief, Mom," he said. "If I eat another bite I'll have to go back to bed for a while." Mary looked down at him with affection.

"Little more sleep wouldn't hurt you none," she said.

"It sure wouldn't hurt me, neither," said Wiley as he sipped the last of his coffee. Nest stood up.

"Which one's Leech's room?" he asked.

"End of the hall," Mary said. "Why?"

"Want to see if he is gone," Nest said.

"Gone?" Mary asked, surprised. "He didn't say anything about leaving. Besides, he's paid up until the end of the month."

"He mentioned something about it on the porch last night," Nest said.

"I'll come along," Wiley said, and Mary watched the two men with suspicion as they walked from her kitchen. She wasn't certain what was going on, but she was certain she didn't like it.

The door at the end of the hall was open, and the room proved to be empty. The bed had not been slept in. In a way Nest was relieved. Wouldn't be good for him to get wounded right now, not with those four evil men out there doing who knows what to other innocent people. He started back down the hall, only to be startled when the door to his old room opened suddenly. Rebecca looked out at him.

"You fixing to shoot me?" she asked, and he realized he had his gun in his hand and couldn't remember drawing it at all.

"Sorry," he mumbled, embarrassed. He must be getting jumpy, but Stacy had always had that effect on him. He reholstered his weapon and followed Rebecca down the stairs. She sure looked nice first thing in the morning.

"He up there?" Mary asked as they came into the kitchen.

"Nope," from Wiley. "He must've pulled out last night. Bed wasn't slept in."

"Huh!" said Mary. "Wonder why?" She looked at Nestor who looked back innocently . . . too innocently.

* * *

Martha was having trouble understanding, having trouble believing the unbelievable. She looked over her horse's head, over her hands securely bound to the saddle horn, at Stacy's back as he rode in the moonlight. He sat up there, comfortable on his horse, straight and tall, picking his way carefully in the dark. She was so stunned, so shocked to her very core, that she had not yet had time for fear or real anger to set in.

He had knocked on her door, and the next thing she knew, she had been tied and gagged and carried effortlessly out of the house while the others slept, unaware of her plight. This big man had carried her like a baby, effortlessly but none too gently. He had sat her up on a horse and now here they were, riding into the prairie, into the night. He had saved her life, or at least her honor, just the other day, and she had trusted him because of that. Now he had done this unbelievable thing and she still didn't know how to feel.

After the first hour, he had removed her gag, which was a big relief to Martha.

"What are you doing?" were the first words out of her mouth.

"Relax," he said. "I'm just taking off your gag so you can breathe better. I have no wish to harm you." He mounted and led her off once more.

"What's going on?" she called to him. "I mean, why did you do this?" He said nothing. She tried again.

"Why?" she asked his back. No response.

"Why?" she called out, louder. He reined in and turned in the saddle until he faced her.

"You won't be hurt, Martha," he said. "Trust me."

"But why are you doing this?" she asked, desperate to find out. Somehow she did not feel afraid of this big brooding man. He sighed clearly in the darkness.

"All in good time, Martha," he said.

"Is it because of Nest?" she asked.

"Has nothing to do with Nest," he said calmly.

"Then why?" she asked again. He took her gag out of his pocket and looked at it.

"Okay," she said. "Okay. I get the idea," and she made up her mind to shut up. A better opportunity for talk would present itself sooner or later. For now all she could do was to comply with the wishes of this man, this unpredictable man. Stacy led her off into the night once more.

The hours clopped away under the horses' hooves, and the moon traveled across the star-speckled sky. The eastern sky turned red behind them, growing lighter and lighter until the sun finally appeared over the horizon. And still they rode. Not fast, but steady, the horses' plodding hooves gradually putting miles of prairie behind them.

Martha was tired. She was tired from not sleeping and she was tired from all the wild emotions that had surged through her and she was tired from sitting on a horse all night. She thought about Nest, about how angry he would be when he discovered she was taken from under his nose. At least she hoped he would be angry.

She thought about kicking her horse suddenly, forcing him to bolt forward. It wouldn't work, though, and she knew it. At best it would only make Stacy angry, and she didn't think making him angry would be a real good idea. Besides, she no longer had any idea which direction would take her back to Fleet, and if she didn't find Fleet right away, there was little likelihood she could survive long enough to find anyplace else.

"Mr. Leech," she finally called softly. He stopped at once and turned his horse. He didn't look the least bit tired. "I need to stop, Mr. Leech," she continued. "Please. Let's just stop for a little while, okay?"

Stacy looked at the young woman. She was tired, real tired, but there was no trace of fear in her eyes.

"Sure thing," he said, and swung down. She watched as he pulled his knife and walked back to her. Somehow it never entered her mind to be afraid of him. He reached up and cut her hands loose, then helped her down. She was very aware of his hands on her waist and a flash of doubt speared through her, but he simply helped her down and then stepped away. For an instant the thought of escape flashed through her mind.

"Don't run off," he said. "Not safe for you out there alone. Besides, I'd find you before you got five miles.'' He said it so calm, so certain. She believed him. She rubbed her wrists where the rope had chafed her, and walked a short distance into the prairie. It was a necessary thing, and she was vaguely surprised when Stacy appeared to pay her no mind as she stepped off into the long grass.

When she returned, he had a small fire going, a coffeepot perched precariously above it. He was starting to go through a saddlebag for more food and cookware.

''Might as well let me do that,'' Martha heard herself say, and Stacy studied her for a moment, then stepped away from the fire. In a way, Martha was surprised at how calmly she was taking her situation. She was proud of how cool and collected she could remain in a potentially dangerous position. Of course, she really had no choice. Besides, if she could gain a little of his trust, sooner or later an opportunity for escape would present itself.

She really wished she had something else to wear besides her nightdress, though. It just didn't seem decent for her to be wearing a nightdress in front of a man, especially in full daylight. Of course, she was properly covered since it was full-length with a tight neck, but it still didn't seem decent, somehow, especially when she was on a horse and some of her legs showed. The coffee water began to boil slowly and she dropped in the proper amount of coffee grounds.

In no time, the coffee was strong and dark, biscuits

were baking in one covered skillet, beans and bacon were cooking in another. She wet her fingers and dripped a few drops of water into the coffee to settle the grounds, then poured a cup and carried it over to where Stacy was sitting on a rock watching her prepare breakfast.

"Much obliged," he said. She nodded and went back to the fire. She would have been more proud of herself if she knew how impressed he was. This young woman had been stolen away in the night, tied to a saddle, and hauled into a place where she was absolutely dependent on her captor for survival. She had the grit and pluck to take it all. She took it, and accepted it, and held herself under tight rein. She was really something for a man to be proud of, that's for sure. If he was her man.

Nest looked over Rusty's head at Wiley riding in the lead as they plodded along. Wiley was one of the best trackers Nest had ever seen, so he wasn't the least bit worried about whether or not they were on the right track. No, he had something else he was worrying over in his mind. Rebecca.

He and Wiley had finished breakfast and packing for the chase when Mom and Rebecca had come out to the barn to say their good-byes. Mom had given him her usual big hug, matching it with another for Wiley. Nest smiled as he remembered Wiley's shuffle-footed embarrassment at the obvious display of affection Mom showed him.

Rebecca had taken Wiley's hand between hers and wished him Godspeed and safety, then turned to Nest. He had reached out his hand to her like Wiley, only she had ignored it and come right on past it and was suddenly wrapping her arms around him in a hug that was just the same as Mom's only a whole lot different. He had been surprised, and hesitated a split second before he hugged her back, pulling her close to him and feeling her full length against him while they stood there in the bright morning sun. He had looked over the girl/woman at Mom and was kind of surprised to find her smiling broadly; was even more surprised when she gave him a small wink over her smile.

All too soon, Rebecca stepped back and turned her face up to him. For an instant that he knew would remain with him for the rest of his life, their eyes locked together.

"Take care, Nestor," she said softly.

"I . . . I will," he answered. Flustered, he had climbed aboard Rusty, back into the world where he was confident and competent. He had looked down on Rebecca, safe from his height. Through sheer force of will, she caught his eyes and locked her gaze to his. She wanted to tell him something and she wanted to be certain he understood.

"Catching those men is not worth your life," she said earnestly.

"I thought you wanted them dead," he said down to her.

"I want you alive more," she said, matter-of-fact. She held his eyes for another second, then turned and walked to the house without looking back. Nest sat there in silence for a second trying to make sense of all that.

"Well, I'll be darned," he had said, almost to himself. His mom had laughed out loud, he still didn't know why.

Rusty sidestepped a small rock and plodded on into the morning. If Nest tried he could still see Rebecca looking up at him; still hear her soft voice. "I want you alive more," she had said, and he worried that around with his mind, trying to find the real meaning. It was only in the first night's camp that it occurred to him to wonder why Martha had not come out to say good-bye.

Yellow Knife lay hidden in the grass, watching the mules pull the two wagons across the prairie. Sixteen mules there were, eight teams, hooked to a chain that led back to the long tongue on the first wagon. The only man he could see was riding the mule just in front of the wagon's left wheel. Every now and then, the mule skinner would reach up and tug on a rope that ran from the bridle of the front mule on the left, all the way back to the top of the first wagon. One pull would make the team turn left; two pulls and they turned right.

Their simple two-man hunting party had once again proven to be more interesting than expected when the team and wagons had showed up. At first, all had been normal, and they bypassed the white man's village and rode toward the setting sun looking for buffalo. They had come across no sign, and were split up, casting about for tracks. Crooked Fist had come back with the tale of the many-mule wagon, and they had been watching it since.

Crooked Fist grinned over at him.

"I think he is alone," he said. "Let us go shoot some arrows into him and see what we can find in his wagons.

"Maybe we should take him prisoner," said Yellow Knife.

"He is wearing a pistol," Crooked Fist pointed out, "and there is a rifle in his saddle." Yellow Knife looked again. Sure enough, a rifle butt protruded from a sheath tied to the man's saddle. He looked at the rifle butt and remembered how one had felt when he had it in his hands.

"Let's do it," he said. They waited until the wagon had gone past, then fell in behind it, easily running up on it from the rear where the man could not see them. Crooked Fist climbed up on the back of the front wagon while it was moving, and made his way to the front where he could look down on the mule skinner.

The rest was so easy that Yellow Knife had trouble believing it.

In a moment, the man lay gasping his life away into the grass while his wagons rolled on, oblivious to his disaster. Yellow Knife looked down on the man. He was lying face down, with Crooked Fist's arrow protruding from the center of his back between his shoulders. There was not a lot of blood, but he seemed unable to move as he gasped each tortured breath. And then he relaxed and was gasping no more.

The wagons trundled on. Yellow Knife studied the dead man. All those years of life ended with something so simple as a wooden arrow with a small stone tip. This man had once been a boy who played with other boys. He had been loved by his family and had grown into a man and maybe been loved by a woman somewhere even though he was so ugly. And now he was no more. He would never move again. Never smile again. And it was all because Crooked Fist, a man he did not know and would never know, shot a small wooden stick into him. Life was very mysterious.

Yellow Knife turned away and ran after the mules. He ran to the front team, seeing the other mules' eyes roll white as he startled each team when he ran past. It was a simple matter to overtake them all and stop the leaders. Once halted, the mules stood patiently in the vast prairie, unaware of the drastic change their life had just taken.

Yellow Knife thought about the man; remembered him gasping his breath into the grass; remembered how easily he had died. Part of him wondered about the man. Did he have a family, a wife maybe, children who would mourn him? He wished he could tell them that their husband and father had died bravely, but really the man had not died bravely. He had died foolishly. A man should know what is happening around him at all times. If he did not, he could easily be killed and that made him something less of a man than a true warrior.

He walked back to the saddled mule the man had been riding. Crooked Fist was yelling in elation at his first kill, and throwing stuff out of the wagon as he went through it. Yellow Knife grinned up at his friend, then put his hand on the smooth rifle butt and pulled it from its sheath.

The rifle was not the same as the one the man called Nest had owned. Yellow Knife had seen rifles like this before. It was the type a few lucky warriors carried, a single shot that required a gate on the top to be opened, and a new cartridge inserted for each shot. It also had to be cocked before it could fire.

At one time such a rifle would have been a prize beyond imagination, something to be wished for in private, something that was too good to ever come true. Now he stood holding that very thing for which he had dared not hope, and he was not satisfied. This rifle was just a nagging reminder of the wonderful lever-action repeating rifle that belonged to the man called Nest.

Crooked Fist called to him from back at the mule skinner's body where he had just stripped the man's pistol belt and strapped it around himself. Yellow Knife grinned at his friend. He could not remember ever seeing Crooked Fist so happy and excited. They came together beside the lead wagon.

"Look!" said Crooked Fist as he held his first scalp high.

"You did well," Yellow Knife said, and watched as his friend's chest swelled with pride.

"Let us cut the mules loose and take them back," Crooked Fist said.

"As you say," Yellow Knife agreed with his friend, and slid his knife out, ready to cut the harness loose. He stopped suddenly.

"Wait," he said. Crooked Fist looked at him curiously.

"Wait for what?"

"What is in these wagons?" Yellow Knife asked.

"The back one is full of food and water for the mules," Crooked Fist answered. "The front one has so many things I cannot describe them all, but we cannot carry them all, either. It would be best to return to the tribe right away so they can come back and take what they want. We will have songs sung about us," he bragged.

"I think we should take the whole wagon back with

us,'' Yellow Knife said. ''Think of the songs they will sing about us if we bring the whole thing back to them.'' Crooked Fist looked at his friend.

''You think you can drive such a wagon?'' he asked.

''I watched him for a long time,'' Yellow Knife responded. ''It did not look so hard.'' Crooked Fist pondered on it for a few minutes. The idea grew in his mind, and soon he smiled at his friend.

''They will sing about us for generations to come,'' he said. Yellow Knife swung into the saddle and looked down on his friend.

''Go and start them moving,'' he said. ''I will see if I can truly drive this thing.'' Crooked Fist picked up the mule skinner's long black whip and walked to the front team. He smacked the front mule with the whip end, and the entire string of mules began to plod forward.

Yellow Knife tugged on the overhead rope two times, then watched in amazement as the long string of mules curved into a right turn. Even more astonishing, as the string turned right, each mule automatically stepped over the long chain which naturally passed underneath them. When he straightened them out with another tug, they stepped over the chain once more as it, too, straightened out. It must have taken the dead mule skinner a long time to train such stupid animals to do that. He must have had a talent with animals. And now the talent was lost forever just because of a small stick with a stone tip that was stuck in his back. Yellow Knife thought that maybe every time a man died some precious talent was lost to the world forever. Maybe the killing of men was not something to be taken too lightly.

Crooked Fist waved his fist in the air and took off running, going after their horses. Yellow Knife waved back and concentrated on keeping the team headed back toward camp.

The white men would doubtless come looking for the mule skinner and wagons someday soon, but Yellow Knife was certain his tribe would take what they wanted from this treasure, and move on long before they could be tracked. Besides, the sky had been darkening off to the west and it was just possible that it would rain and wash out their tracks altogether. He wished they had thrown the muleskinner's body on the wagon. Maybe the white men would never find him if they had. Of course, maybe they would never find him anyway.

The mules did not go very fast. It was obvious that they would not get back to the tribe until the next night, but when they did, there would be a feast to end all feasts and the names of Yellow Knife and Crooked Fist would be something the storytellers would talk about for generations to come.

The mules plodded on. Yellow Knife concentrated on keeping them going in the right direction. After a while a sound from behind made him turn.

Crooked Fist was gazing down at him from the wagon, bow drawn.

"Ho!" he said. "You would not be much harder to kill than he was." Yellow Knife could say nothing, but he was shamed. His friend had come up behind him and had he not been his friend, could have killed him just as easily as the mule skinner had been killed. He knew he had just learned the lesson of a warrior, but that did not make it taste any better. Nobody would ever sneak up on him again. He was learning fast, and would someday be a great warrior.

If he lived.

Chapter Eight

Martha was flat worn out. All day they had ridden, eating beef jerky in the saddle as they plodded across the prairie. Always heading west. Toward the wilderness.

Two hours before sundown, Leech had finally pulled to a halt in a small dead-end arroyo.

"We'll camp here," he announced. Martha slid down from her horse and it was all she could do to keep from plopping into a frazzled puddle right there on the ground. Her knees ached deep and steady, but her rear end ached even more. She was not used to long hours in a saddle. It would be so easy for her to wilt into a crumpled mess of girl right there on the ground, but she refused to let him see her weakness. She untied the bag of food and got out the coffeepot.

Stacy watched the young woman. He knew how tired she must be, he was tired himself, but she refused to complain or let him see her fatigue. He had been right about her. Now if he only had enough time to show her what he wanted to show her. Their time was limited, he had no doubt. Somewhere behind, Nest was probably coming along after them, fire in his eyes.

Stacy expertly got their small cooking fire started, then saw to the animals for the night. It was a good place to camp, at least for out in the prairie. The animals could be picketed behind the camp, free to wander and eat without possibility of escape or theft. The only real way they could be assaulted was from the front, although it would be possible for someone to shoot down on them from the arroyo banks. *If* they were discovered camping there. It was Stacy's plan that they not be discovered.

He took blankets and made up his bedroll. It was going to be cold during the night and they would not have a fire. He only made up one bedroll. It was all the blankets he had.

He looked over at Martha as she struggled with maintaining her modesty while she cooked. If her abduction had been a planned thing, he would have figured how to bring her clothes. But it hadn't been a planned thing, not really. It had just sort of happened, spur of the moment, and now here she was and he was responsible. He took his pair of clean pants and his clean plaid shirt from the saddlebags. He took off his leather vest and added it to the pile, then carried the clothes over to her.

"Here, Martha," he said. "Put these on." She looked him in the eye for a moment, then took the bundle of clothes. He tried a small smile.

"You may not be real stylish," he said, "but at least you won't have to worry about your modesty." He wanted her to smile back, wanted her to show some sign of weakening her resolve against him, but she did not change expression.

"I will wear them," she said. It was all she said. She walked back behind the horses and Stacy tended the fire. The fire really didn't need any tending, but it was something to do instead of thinking about her changing into his own clothes back there. It would have been easy for him to look and see her. He did not look.

Martha changed clothes as rapidly as she could, watching Leech all the while. He appeared to pay her no mind, appeared to have no interest in her whatsoever. She was relieved. She was also curious. What did the man want with her? Why would he take such a big chance to steal her away? What could he hope to gain?

The shirt went on right over her nightdress and she carefully buttoned each and every button down the front. The trousers were much too large both around the waist and in length. Martha took two of the pretty blue ribbons from her nightdress, twisted them into a rough rope and threaded them through the belt loops. She pulled them tight and tied them off. There. That should keep the trousers up securely. She rolled up the legs until they would not interfere with her walking . . . or running. The leather vest was the final touch, and she felt at least decently covered, if not very attractive.

Stacy smiled up at her when she walked back to the fire. She did not smile back. He looked into her face. Her face was hard, suspicious, guarded. He did not blame her. He wanted to tell her how cute she was in his clothes. Wanted her to know how much she looked like a little girl, what with everything being way too big for her. He didn't think it would be a good idea. She was not in the mood for pleasantries.

"Coffee's almost done," he said. Martha knelt down by the fire and resumed cooking the dinner. More beans, only with potatoes this time.

"Why don't you go and shoot something to eat?" she asked. He studied her.

"Can't risk the noise," he finally explained. "Not yet, anyway. Maybe tomorrow." She stirred the beans and looked up at him.

"They're coming anyway, you know," she said. It was not a question. "It's just a matter of time and they'll catch us." She waited for him to speak.

"Not worried about them," he said. "Can't risk the noise because of the Indians. Might be almost anywhere around here.'' He saw her startled expression and the flash of fear that she quickly controlled.

Martha hadn't thought about Indians. There hadn't been any big trouble with them for quite a while, at least not that she knew about. Still, out here they were at the Indians' mercy if they were caught, and the Indians weren't particularly known for their mercy. She didn't want to think about it. She became aware that he was studying her.

''You don't have to worry,'' he said. ''Long as you do what I say when I say it, you'll be fine. I have been living out here for a long time,'' he added, ''and I still have *my* hair.''

She wanted to believe him. She waited for him to say more. Finally it became apparent he was not going to say anything else. Time to change the subject.

''Why don't you tell me what this is all about,'' she suggested.

''All in good time,'' he said. It was the same thing he had said in the morning so long ago. Martha pondered on that. She did not doubt for a moment that this big man had taken her for a reason, and she wanted to figure out what the reason could be. The answer flooded over her like lightning.

''You want them to come after us,'' she said accusingly. ''You want them to come after us because you want them to catch us.'' She looked him hard in the eye. ''You want Nest, don't you? You want him to come after us and you want him angry and then you want to kill him.''

She turned away from him, not wanting him to see the fear in her face. There was no doubt in her mind that this big, quiet man was going to get his way. Nest would come. Nest would be angry. And this big man could and would kill him dead. She had seen him in action. He was cool, calm, and ever so fast with that big handgun. She didn't know whether to hope Nest was coming or not.

Nest was coming all right, but it was merely by accident. Wiley was tracking the four killers. He was kind of annoyed by the two riders whose tracks had covered the killers, but he could still follow along okay.

''These two are headed north too,'' he said. Nest grunted an acknowledgment. He wondered briefly about the two, then dismissed them from his mind. He didn't care who they were. It was the four ahead of them he was after. Rusty stepped across the prairie while they looked for a place to camp.

''They keep going this way, we'll be in Beaver in two days,'' Wiley added.

''Wonderful.'' Beaver was the last stop before true wilderness. A mere hovel of sod, it boasted the worst food, the worst whiskey, and the scruffiest patrons. Every miserable villain in the area had been known to stop there at one time or another. In a way it was logical that the killers would head for there, too.

The place was run by the filthiest man Nest could ever recall seeing. He was called Buff, but his real name was unknown and likely to stay that way. Probably had some horrible past to drive him to such a desolate, lonely place, and Nest had no desire to find out what it was.

Buff was about six feet tall, didn't matter whether he was standing up or lying down. He was a huge, solid block of a man, the type that ignorant folks figured was massively fat. Only it was muscle, hard and unforgiving, that made up his great bulk. Those who broke his few rules found that out suddenly and harshly, for there was no mercy in the man. He would crush the offender without emotion, like it was nothing personal, just business. Those he crushed took it personal though, because he was so strong and so efficient at maintaining discipline and he did it as quickly and effortlessly as possible for himself. That usually meant crippling his opponent, changing their lives forever in the twinkling of an eye. Nest had met several with limps or deformed arms who had transgressed at Beaver. None wanted to tangle with Buff ever again.

Wiley swung down.

"Here's where the killers camped," he said. "Other two kept going. This spot looks as good as any to me." Nest looked down on his friend.

"You want to quit already?" he asked in mock surprise. The sun was setting big and red in the west. ''We haven't hardly got started yet.'' Wiley looked up at him.

''Figured I'd clean my weapons while there's still some light,'' he lied as he stripped the saddle from his horse.

''Cleaning your guns is a waste of time,'' said Nest. ''Better you should get a big rock or something.'' He swung down and stripped the saddle.

''Now, there you go again,'' Wiley complained. ''How many times have I saved your miserable life, and what thanks do I get? None. Just complaints about my shooting ability.''

''Not your ability I complain about,'' said Nest. ''It's your lack of it that bothers me. Every time you pull that Colt, I have the urge to run out in front of you on account of that is the safest place to be.'' Wiley snorted a laugh.

''Someday you will regret making fun of me,'' he said. ''Someday my shooting skills will save your miserable life.''

''Be sure they spell my name right on the stone,'' Nest responded as he spread his bedroll. Wiley smiled at his friend. He already had the coffeepot going on the small, smokeless fire.

Jubil lay in his bedroll and looked up at the stars. Going to get pretty cold this night, he was thinking.

The horses were tied to the picket line, secure for

the night, and Amos and Webb were already down in their bedrolls. Reb was finishing up putting the fire out for good.

Jubil played with the idea of posting a guard, but they were pretty well hidden in one of the small arroyos, and the only way they could be discovered in the dark would be if someone stumbled over them. Last time they laid up in an arroyo, the Indians had gone right on by. Nope. No guard necessary, at least not this night. They all slept with their guns handy anyway.

He watched the stars and thought about where he was and with whom. He seemed to think the same things before he went to sleep each night, always being surprised at how different life was from what it had once been. It had been so nice back in their little rented house, sleeping in that small, soft bed with his pretty wife. Now he was back under the stars, out in the weather again. At least when he was in the army he had slept in a big tent.

He listened as Reb slid into his own bedroll, and then the sounds of the night moved in. He was satisfied. A person could walk within ten feet of the camp and never know it was there if he didn't hear the horses tearing at the prairie grass. Tomorrow they would be at Beaver where they could stock up on supplies and relax for a day before heading out once more. Jubil wondered how many people were out there tonight sleeping alive and warm, who would be dead after his men got done with their next hunting trip.

The small sliver of the moon cast very little light on the still forms of the four sleeping men.

"Surely you don't expect us to sleep in the same bedroll?" Martha asked, shocked to the center of her being. Stacy was finishing the last of the coffee, squatting down by the dying embers of the small fire. It was the first she had noticed there was only one place to sleep. He sighed.

"Only have one and it is going to get cold," he explained laconically. He could see her shocked expression even in the dark.

"I will stay by the fire," Martha declared firmly.

"Not going to be any fire," he came back.

"If it is too much trouble for you, I'll keep it going," she said. He looked over his cup at her.

"Indians can smell a fire for miles," he explained. That stopped her for a moment. She could see the sense in that.

"You will have all those clothes on, and I give you my word you will not be bothered," he added with finality. The conversation was over as far as he was concerned.

"I won't do it," she declared. Martha watched him shrug.

"Suit yourself," he said, like it didn't make any difference to him. She didn't understand him at all. He seemed so disinterested in her, almost like he was only half aware she was even there. He certainly wasn't like those silly young men back in Fleet, all fumble-footed whenever they were around her.

Stacy scattered the few glowing coals, and she watched in dismay as the little glimmers of red slowly faded. He unstrapped his gun belt and crawled into the bedroll. He had his gun under his hand as he lay there. Somehow she knew that was the way he slept every night out in the wild.

The last little ember flared and was gone and Martha felt more alone than she had ever felt in her entire life. Alone and exhausted. She could feel the cold begin to seep through her clothes. She was always a practical girl, and she reasoned it out while she sat there and shivered. She had to survive and to do that she had to be strong and awake. That meant she had to get as much sleep as possible and take good care of herself. Only way to do that was for her to go to bed. There was only one bed and Leech was in it.

She listened as his breathing evened out. She could hardly feel her fingers, they were so cold. He hadn't moved in ever so long, she was certain he was asleep. She sighed, then got to her feet and went over to the bedroll. She slid under the blanket, tucking the end of it between her and the ground. At once the warmth from the motionless man soaked into her. He didn't move and she was very careful not to touch him as she lay there. Almost immediately, she could feel the waves of long-denied sleep flood over her.

"Knew you were a smart girl," he said softly, and she stared into the night for a second, then allowed her eyes to close and was asleep.

The smell of something wonderful wormed into her brain. What was it? Coffee? That was it. Coffee. Now why could she smell coffee in the middle of the night, and how come she was getting cold all of a sudden? She opened her eyes.

It was growing light in the east, and Stacy . . . Mr. Leech . . . was hunched down by the fire pouring coffee into one of the metal cups. He brought it over to her and handed it down. To Martha there seemed something slightly decadent about having coffee in bed, but she decided right away that she liked it.

"Thank you," she said after her first sip. It was actually pretty good coffee.

"Morning," was his response. He went back to the fire, poured himself a cup, and squatted by the fire. He took a sip and nested the cup in his hands, warming his fingers.

"How'd you sleep?" he asked quietly.

"Fine," she said. "I slept fine." It was the first she had thought about the two of them being together in the same bed, and she grew angry with herself as she felt a flush come over her face. She could swear she saw a twinkle of humor in his eyes, and it did not help her disposition any to think he might be laughing at her. She rolled out of bed angrily.

"You know," she said through gritted teeth, "when Nest catches up with you I hope he puts you in jail for a hundred years." Leech looked startled. One eyebrow raised in surprise.

"Have I offended you in some way?" he asked. "Maybe you don't like coffee or something."

"Have you offended me?" she asked, then repeated, "Have you offended me?" She shook her finger at him. "First you steal me away from my home without even allowing me to get dressed properly. You stick me on a horse and drag me out on the prairie going who knows where. You won't tell me where we're going or why you took me. You make me wear these ridiculous clothes just to maintain a semblance of decency, and to top it all off, you force me to spend the night in the same bed with you! I guess you could say you have offended me. Yes. I believe you have offended me, all right!"

"But aside from that, it's been okay, hasn't it?" he asked. The corners of his mouth turned up in a slight smile.

Martha looked down on him, astonished. He was most definitely laughing at her! She made to walk past him, only swung her hips into his shoulder. His cup went flying, and he tumbled onto the ground. She looked down on him, waiting for his anger to come. She was amazed to see that he was laughing instead.

"Don't hold back," he said as he laughed. "Let me know how you really feel."

Martha glared down at him as he brushed ineffectively at the coffee spilled on his jeans. She tried to stay angry, tried to remember the red-hot frustration that had driven her to action. He sat there on the ground laughing up at her, looking like a silly little boy. In spite of herself she felt her mouth turn up in a smile and then she was laughing too.

Chapter Nine

Buff shaded his eyes with a meaty hand, and watched the four riders pick their way down the small bluff to the east. Customers. He allowed a small smile to curl the corner of his mouth. More scum of the earth coming to see him and spend some of their ill-gotten gains. He shrugged. No business of his how they got their money. He went inside, made sure the sawed-off Greener shotgun behind the bar was loaded, and wiped the dust from the bar. He was wiping off the glasses when the door opened and they came in.

First one through the door was Amos. Buff didn't know his last name and couldn't care less. Amos was one of his least favorite people, almost too awful for even Buff to tolerate. He was followed by the other three, Jubil bringing up the rear.

124

"Whiskey," said Amos. Buff stood and looked at him from over the bar until Amos got the idea and slapped a silver dollar down on the scarred wood.

"I got money," he declared.

Buff planted a glass in front of him and poured it full of his homemade liquor. He watched Amos toss it back and slap down the glass, ready for more. Buff marveled at the hardness of the old man, for he neither blinked nor showed any other signs of the harshness of the beverage.

It was harsh and that was a fact. Buff made it himself, starting with a barrel of pure alcohol to which he added mostly everything unpleasant he could find around at the time. Chewing tobacco was in there, along with some snake heads, hot peppers, and such. He scooped it out of the old barrel, usually holding his nose and breathing as little as possible, and funneled it into bottles. So far nobody had died from drinking it. Bound to happen sooner or later, though.

Actually, he was starting to run low on pure alcohol, but Stubby Barnes was due through here with his jerkline team pretty soon, so he wasn't worried. He splashed the glass full and Amos slugged it down once more.

"Me, too," said Webb as he laid a dollar on the bar. He tossed back his glass, and Buff watched the young man as his eyes watered and his face turned red. He finally got back under control and put his glass back on the bar.

"Good," he said. "Again." Buff almost smiled. Men could be so stupid sometimes. He poured another glass and carefully took the money from the bar. All his business was cash only. No trusting his customers, and that was a fact.

Jubil and Reb ignored the bar, went over and sat down at the only table. It was by the single window in the room, and the morning light splashed on the scarred wood. The table had seen lots of villains in its day and, in fact, a man had died on it just about a year ago. He was planted out back somewhere, Buff was no longer quite certain where.

"How about some coffee and food," Jubil said. Buff nodded and began to open a can of beans.

"You want 'em hot or cold?" he asked. Jubil looked disgusted.

"Hot, of course," he said. "With some meat, too, and maybe some potatoes."

"Take about a hour and a half," Buff said.

"That will be all right," said Jubil. "We are planning to stay the day." Buff shrugged. Didn't matter to him one way or the other. He took note of where the whiskey level was in the bottle and turned to build a fire in the small fireplace. He was not surprised to hear the faint clink of the bottle on glass behind him. With the kind of customers his place attracted, it was always the same.

* * *

The breakfast was over, the fire was out, and the horses were saddled. All signs of their camp had carefully been eliminated by Stacy, and Martha had to admit she was impressed. He was so sparing in his actions, so confident and competent in the wilderness, that she no longer feared for her safety. He could obviously take care of them both. She stood there, waiting for him to tell her to mount up. She was rather tender in her southern region, and was not anxious to plant herself in the saddle once more, at least not any sooner than she had to.

Stacy was fumbling around in his saddlebag, then turned and came over to her, a rolled gun belt and holstered pistol in his hand. He held it out to her.

"Here," he said. "Put this on." She looked at him for a moment, wide-eyed. He motioned with the belt.

"Here," he repeated. "It's not a snake. It won't hurt you. Put it on."

She reached out and took the gun belt. It was surprisingly heavy, what with the blue steel pistol and numerous brass cartridges. She swung it around her as she had seen him do, and belted it on. The pistol hung heavy on her right hip, and the whole thing felt awkward and very heavy to her.

"You know how to use one of those?" he asked. Martha shook her head. She had been carefully shielded from the world of firearms. In fact, this was the first one she had ever handled. Stacy sighed.

"Okay," he said. "First thing is to learn how to

load and unload. Take it out of the holster, but be careful on account of it is loaded.'' Martha looked at him.

''You are trusting me with a loaded gun?'' she asked. He shrugged.

''You should have a means of defending yourself out here,'' he explained. ''Besides, you would not want to use it on me. You need me to stay alive, re-member?'' he pointed out in case she had forgotten. She nodded.

''I'll be glad when Nest catches up with you,'' she said, angry at her helplessness.

''We'll worry about that when it happens,'' he re-sponded calmly. ''For now, pay attention on account of I don't want to have to say this twice. Take out the gun.''

Martha pulled the heavy thing from the holster. It felt really big in her hand, big and heavy, almost heavy enough so it took two hands to hold it securely.

In spite of what he said, Stacy was very patient during the next hour as he showed her the basics of gun handling. She unloaded it, and he showed her how to dry-fire it, explaining how she should wait until her target got real close and then aim for the middle of whatever she wanted to shoot.

''Don't jerk the trigger,'' he said. ''Just squeeze it nice and easy. Chances are, if the gun surprises you when it goes off, it will be a good shot.'' She held it out in front of her with both hands, thumbed back the jagged hammer, and clicked into the prairie until he was satisfied.

"Guess that'll do," he finally said. "Load up and we'll be on our way." Martha slid the shiny brass bullets into the gun one by one. They felt heavy and somehow deadly as they dropped into the cylinder. She snapped the gate closed and dropped the gun into her holster. It still felt strange to have that extra weight around her waist. Somehow, it also felt lethal, and she had a sense of confidence that she hadn't had earlier. At least she could defend herself if she had to.

It never entered her mind that she might have to defend herself from Stacy. He had proven himself safe beyond question, as far as she was concerned. Nope. The gun might come in handy against animals or Indians, but not against him.

The stirrup was pretty high, and he put his hands on her waist and effortlessly lifted her to the horse's back.

"What's his name?" she asked. He looked up at her, and she could easily see the twinkle in his eye.

"His name is Mabel," he said. She blushed. She hadn't noticed it was a mare. He was still grinning as he mounted his horse. She was still blushing, too.

The afternoon was half gone when Stacy reined in on the bluff overlooking the Beaver Station. He was not pleased to see the four horses in the corral.

"Oh, look!" said Martha as she reined in beside

him. "A house." Stacy smiled grimly and turned to
her.

"That is true enough," he said, "but do not think
that is a home." She looked puzzled, and he went on.
He couldn't remember the last time he had talked so
much to anyone.

"That is probably one of the most evil establish-
ments on the frontier. It is run by a villain who caters
to villains. A man can get robbed or killed or worse
down there, and he would just disappear, never to be
heard from again. It is a place to keep your back to a
wall and your opinions to yourself." Martha looked
suitably impressed.

"Are we stopping here?" she asked.

"We need supplies," he said flatly. "Because it is
such an evil place, I will not take you down there with
me. I would ask that you stay back on the other side
of the ridge until I return with what we need."

"Now wait a minute," she said, agitated. "You told
me earlier that I needed you to survive out here. While
I wish it were not true, it is a fact. I have no idea
where we are, no idea how to get home, and no idea
how to stay alive out here. You cannot leave me while
you go down to someplace that is so bad you may
never return. The idea of slowly starving to death is
worse than anything that may or may not happen down
there. Besides, there may be Indians about." She
looked him full in the eye while he sat there and studied on what she had said.

"Thought you were so sure Nest is right behind us," he said after a moment.

"He is," Martha replied firmly.

"Then you won't mind waiting up here," Stacy said.

"I will not stay behind," she stated. He sighed.

"Okay," he said. "Only I think those four horses down there belong to the friends of the man I killed in town. It would probably be best if they believe we are married. Man's liable to think twice before he goes up against an angry husband," he added. Martha hesitated.

"Do you think they will be out for vengeance?" she asked.

"No. I think the death of one of them means almost nothing to the others. They probably had his belongings divided before they got him to the doctor's place." Martha looked at him doubtfully. He shrugged.

"People can be pretty hard out here," he explained. "Especially bad people. Don't forget these are the men who killed Rebecca's parents without batting an eye." He turned to ride down, then turned back.

"Take the thong off the hammer of your gun, keep your back to a wall, and watch them all the time," he said. "If you find it necessary to shoot, remember to hold on their middle and do not hesitate to pull the trigger on account of they will not give you a second chance." With that cryptic advice he turned and they

started down the bluff. Martha could feel the worry
gnawing at her insides. Surely it couldn't be as bad as
he said. He was probably just trying to scare her into
silent submission. He had succeeded in scaring her,
that was certain.

All too soon they reined in at the front of the sod
house. Stacy swung down, unfastened the thong from
his gun and wrapped the reins around the flimsy hitching rail. Martha took a deep breath and swung down.
She handed him the reins and he loose-tied her horse
just like his. He looked pointedly at her pistol, and she
reluctantly reached down and took off the thong. She
could not ever imagine using the evil thing against
another human being. Stacy pulled on the latchstring
and went inside. Martha followed.

All the men inside had heard them ride up, and although they looked casual enough, there was an air of
tension in the place that was easy to feel. When Martha walked in, she could almost feel the sudden sharp-
ness of the men's attention. In spite of herself, she
wanted to stay close to Leech. Better the devil she
knew, than the one she didn't.

"Howdy, Stacy," said the huge man behind the bar.
Stacy nodded and went to the end of the short bar,
leaving just enough room for Martha between him and
the wall. Martha fitted herself in there while the other
men watched their every move. Stacy leaned his back
on the bar and gazed back.

"You want a drink?" asked the man behind the bar.

"No thanks, Buff," said Stacy. "Just stopped for some supplies. How you fixed?"

"Got some," Buff responded. "Tell me what you need and I'll tell you what I have left. Jerkline ain't been through yet," he added.

"I smell coffee and food," Stacy observed. He never took his eyes off the other men.

"Fixin' grub for these folks," Buff said. "Can fix you some too, if'n you want."

"No time," Stacy said. "Coffee would be good, though."

" 'Kay." Buff turned to the coffeepot. The old man at the bar moved slightly.

"She's a real good looker," he said to Stacy, indicating Martha with a nod of his head. Stacy gazed at the dirty old man.

"Leave my wife out of this," he said. "You remember what happened to the last man who tried anything with her." The old man held up his hands.

"Didn't mean nothin', Mister," he whined. "Just stating a fact, that was all." He tried a smile, but it came off as a nasty grin, showing stubs of rotting yellow teeth. Martha thought he was the most repulsive human being she had ever seen. There was a younger man at the bar too, and he was looking at her with bright eyes, but saying nothing. It made her uncomfortable.

"Boys, let her be," came softly from the man at the table, and suddenly he had Martha's attention. He was an older man, almost fatherly in appearance. The way the two men at the bar deferred to him, it was clear he was the leader of the group. He gazed back at her calmly.

"Thank you," she heard herself say.

"Don't believe a lady should be bothered by scum such as they," he said in the same soft voice. Martha found herself wanting to trust him, but she thought about Rebecca's parents and was silent.

"You headed west?" he asked casually.

"Got a ranch," Stacy said before she could answer. "We're headed home."

"Nice to have a home," Jubil said. "West of here, is it?"

Stacy shrugged his head toward the door.

"Out there a piece," he said. Jubil smiled.

"Man can't be too careful, huh?" he asked.

"Don't think so," was Stacy's laconic reply.

Mary was beside herself. Nest and Wiley were long gone before she discovered that Martha was missing. Worse, her bed had not been slept in, and that meant she had been missing all night. Hard as it was for Mary to accept, the situation was obvious. Stacy Leech had stolen her almost-daughter away, stolen her and disappeared into the vast, uncaring prairie.

Rebecca set a cup of tea in front of the distraught woman. "I don't understand it," Rebecca said. "He seemed so nice. He even killed a man for her only the day before.'' She sat down at the table with Mary.

''I knew he liked her,'' Mary said softly, hating herself for being so blind. ''I knew it, but I thought maybe he was here on account of Nestor. I thought he was coming to what had been his hometown to maybe make up for the trouble he had caused back when he was a youngster.'' She shook her head in dismay. ''I never once thought he was evil enough to steal Martha away like that.'' She sipped at her tea without tasting it or even being aware she was doing it. ''I never thought he was *that* bad.'' Rebecca looked across the table at the suffering woman. Mary suddenly looked so much older.

''Maybe,'' she said, ''if he really loves her, he will treat her well.''

''Won't matter none,'' Mary came back. ''When Nestor finds out, there will be no place Stacy can hide.'' She sighed. ''Nestor will kill him for sure.''

Rebecca bit her lip and looked out the window. Small clouds floated in the blue afternoon sky.

''Nestor loves her, then?'' she asked. Mary's face took on the first sign of life Rebecca had seen since the discovery of Martha's disappearance. She looked across the table at Rebecca, eyes bright.

''Don't worry, honey,'' Mary said. ''You got him if you want him. He loves her like a sister, nothing more.'' She looked out the window too, then went on, almost to herself. ''Martha thought she loved him, though. 'Course she didn't, least not real grown-up love. It's just that they were sort of pushed together, you know. And there aren't that many good men out in this country. Not enough for a young girl to pick from, you know what I mean.'' She lapsed into silence, and the two women sat there, each lost in her own thoughts. It almost startled Rebecca when Mary broke the quiet.

''Sure wish I could get word to Nestor,'' she said. Rebecca raised her eyebrows and looked across the table at her new friend.

''We ought to make Beaver Station just after nightfall,'' Wiley said as the two men rested on their horses. ''My guess is they're going to be there when we get there.'' Nest thought about that for a minute.

''Don't really care to come up on them while they are inside that place,'' he said. ''It's almost like a fort, and with all the supplies in there they could hold out a lot longer than we could.'' Wiley sighed and looked at the reddening horizon.

''Good spot to camp 'bout ten minutes ahead,'' he said, then kicked his horse into motion and led off toward the setting sun.

Nest followed along behind. He couldn't seem to get that girl out of his mind, and he wasn't quite sure why. When she had been around all the time, back when they were out at her folks' wagon, he had paid her hardly no mind at all. Now, he kept trying to remember exactly what her face looked like when she smiled, how her eyes looked when she was serious. He should be paying attention to the job at hand. Lord knew, it was dangerous enough when a man was paying attention.

Wiley reined in, and Nest looked over the selected campsite. It met with his approval. 'Course, when was the last time Wiley had ever picked a site that wasn't well thought out? Nest swung down from Rusty and began to loosen the saddle. He wondered what Rebecca was doing that very minute.

Martha was almost frantic. The big man called Buff was just about finished putting their supplies in a bag, and in a few minutes she and Stacy would be on their way to who knows where. There would be no possibility of escape from him once they were out in the prairie once more. On the other hand, her only hope lay in the hands of men who might very well be the murderers of Rebecca's parents, and who knows how many others.

Buff tied the bag closed and laid it on the bar.

"There you are," he said to Stacy. "Should be enough to last you a while." Stacy nodded and put a twenty-dollar gold piece on the bar. Buff slid it into his meaty fingers and it disappeared somewhere in his crusty clothing. Three silver dollars in change clanked onto the bar. Stacy pocketed the change and slung the bag over his left shoulder, keeping his right hand free.

"See you," he said, and started across the short distance to the door.

"He isn't my husband," Martha said suddenly. Stacy stopped as if shot, and she definitely had the attention of everyone in the room. Desperate, she went on.

"He has stolen me away from my home and is taking me to I don't know where." Nobody moved. Stacy just looked solid and resigned.

"I need help," Martha went on. "If any of you will help me, I will pay you when I get back home."

She didn't understand why nobody said anything, why nobody *did* anything.

"I don't have a lot of money," she continued desperately, speaking very fast, "but I will give you what I have if you just get me home." Stacy easy-stepped over to the other corner where he could keep an eye on everyone in the room, including her. He didn't look worried or upset, and that surprised her some. He just looked ready and patient, waiting for whatever was to come.

"That true, Mister?" asked Jubil quietly. Stacy's answer was soft, so soft that Martha had to strain to hear him.

"You boys had best mind your own business," he said. His hand dropped to his gun butt, and his voice got harsh. "Buff," he said, "if your hand drops below that bar, I'm gonna figure you are taking a hand in this." Buff carefully reversed his movement and placed both meaty hands on the bar. The old man at the end cackled suddenly. He was almost drooling, and not at all sober. Martha stared at him in fascination.

''Hey, mister,'' he said, ''If she ain't your wife, I got three dollars left. Don't suppose you'd consider selling her for a while.''

Stacy looked over at the old man and glanced at Martha.

''Three dollars, huh,'' he finally said. ''Let's see it.'' Martha was shocked to her very core. Shocked and horrified. She watched the old man like a bird might watch a snake, disgusted by him, yet unable to look away. The old man wiped his nose with his sleeve and pulled three silver dollars from his coat pocket.

''Here 'tis,'' he said. ''Three good American dollars.'' He bit one to show it was real, and Martha watched his yellow tooth stubs clink on the silver. When he took the dollar down, a string of drool stretched from his mouth to the coin, but he appeared not to notice.

''Stacy,'' she said, completely forgetting that this was all brought about by her doing. ''For God's sake, Stacy,'' she repeated. He appeared to be considering the old man's offer. He looked from the three dollars to her several times.

''Nope,'' he finally said. ''Can't do it. She's a lot of trouble, but I'm gettin' used to having her around.'' The old man looked disappointed and Martha began to breathe once more. Stacy put the bag on the floor, watching the others carefully as he did.

"Martha," he said to her hard. "Fetch this bag out to the horses. I'll be along shortly." Ordinarily Martha would have rebelled at his tone of voice without even thinking about it, but the sight of the old man watching her with rheumy eyes silenced any objections she might have had. Obediently she walked to the bag and picked it up. She felt Stacy slip her heavy gun from its holster as she did so.

"Take it outside," he said to her again, and she carried the heavy bag out the door and into the fresh evening air. She was shaking inside, and felt like she had just escaped from something so horrible she couldn't even begin to imagine. She could easily hear the rest of the conversation from through the open door.

Inside, the man at the table looked at Stacy.

"You really steal her?" Jubil asked. Stacy looked across the room at him.

"Mister," he said. "You been doing really good up to now. Be a shame to spoil it." Jubil shrugged. Who was he to question somebody else? At first the woman had reminded him of someone, but that wore off real quick when he remembered just how fast and willing this big man was with his gun.

"No skin off my nose," Jubil finally said. The big man walked carefully to the door, the girl's gun in one hand, his other hand hovering over his own gun. Nobody made any move to stop him.

Chapter Ten

Martha felt like every bone in her hips was slowly coming unhooked from its neighbors. Besides that, it felt like all the skin in that particular portion of her anatomy had been flayed off. Every movement of the horse hurt. They had been riding steadily since leaving that awful sod house. Now it was well into dark and she was flat exhausted.

"Mr. Leech?" she finally said. "Are we going to ride all night?"

"The name is Stacy," came floating back from the dark form ahead. Silence dragged on as they plodded into the dark.

"Stacy?" she finally said. "Can we stop pretty soon?" He reined in at once and swung down.

"Sure thing," he said as he came over and helped

141

her down. It felt unbelievably wonderful to be standing on solid ground once more. She looked around as she stretched her weary muscles and yawned. They were in another of the many arroyos in this part of the country. They all looked the same, chest-high and looking like nothing so much as a V-shaped slash in the prairie. She had no idea how a body kept from being lost out here.

Stacy handed her some jerky.

"Here," he said. "No fire tonight."

"No fire?" she asked petulantly. She had been thinking about coffee for what seemed like hours.

"Remember those men at Beaver?" he asked. Martha shuddered inside.

"No fire," she agreed. She gnawed on the jerky, finally working off a bite-sized piece. It was better than nothing, only it sure took a long time to chew.

Stacy made up the bedroll.

"There," he said. "You can lie down there if you've a mind to. I'll see to the horses." He took the animals to the back of the arroyo and began to fuss with them. Martha dropped on the bedroll, pulled the blanket up to her neck. She eased her head down on the saddle and somehow the smell of horse and leather was comforting. She wanted to go right to sleep but didn't dare. She sighed. She would have to stay awake until he fell asleep, again.

Stacy finished up with the horses and yawned. He was tired, so he had no doubt poor Martha was exhausted. Maybe he would let her sleep in the morning. Probably wouldn't hurt the horses any, either. He was reasonably certain the men from the Beaver Station couldn't find them that soon. If they chose to look for them.

He walked over to the huddled form in the bedroll and looked down on her. Her breathing was even and steady, the deep breathing of a person fast asleep. He reached down and took the jerky from where she still clutched it in her hand. She did not move at all, and he tucked the food back in the cloth bag and stuffed it into the saddle bag lying there by her head. He gently adjusted the blanket over her still form, took off his gun belt, and crawled in beside her, being careful not to touch her.

Stacy rested on one elbow and looked down on her. He reached up a hand and brushed back some of her hair from her face. He lightly rested his hand on her hair for a moment, then took his pistol to hand, rolled over and put his head down on the saddle next to hers.

"Good night, Martha," he said softly. Of course he got no reply, nor did he expect any from the sleeping young woman. He sighed and felt the tiredness of the long, hard day soak into him. The Colt felt solid and good in his hand as he allowed his eyes to ease closed, secure in the knowledge that the horses would warn them of any danger. Sleep crept over him.

"Good night, Stacy," she said softly, only half awake. His eyes snapped open and he stared into the night for a moment before once more drifting into sleep.

"Them four pulled out a couple hours ago," Buff said. He carefully kept his hands above the bar. He didn't trust lawmen, and did not want to give them any opportunity to gun him down.

"Which way they go?" Nest asked.

"Don't know for sure," Buff answered. "North, I think." Nest nodded.

"Okay, thanks," he said. Buff looked at the two lawmen. Couldn't hurt to get on their good side.

"I figure they might have been following that other couple," he volunteered. Nest and Wiley looked interested.

"The other couple?" Wiley asked.

"Yeah," said Buff. "Man named Stacy Leech and his woman." Nest looked surprised.

"His woman?" he wanted to know. Buff nodded.

"Yup," he said. "Pretty thing. Not too old, neither."

"What did she look like?" Nest asked. Where in the world had Stacy found a woman out here?

"Kinda light hair. Dressed in man's clothes."

"Man's clothes?" Wiley asked. Buff was pleased. He had obviously gotten the lawmen's attention.

"Yeah," he said. "You know, trousers too long and rolled up at the bottom; shirt way too big for her; vest that practically hung down to her knees." He looked away from the two men and pictured her in his mind. "Kinda cute in all them big clothes, you know?" he added.

Wiley shook his head. "Well, if that don't beat all," he said. "Imagine finding a woman out here."

"Yeah," said Nest. "He always did have a lucky streak."

"Didn't find her, I don't think," Buff volunteered. He sure had their attention again.

"What d'ya mean by that?" Wiley asked.

"She said he stole her," Buff said flatly. The lawmen's eyebrows raised in surprise, all four of them. It was almost comical, but Buff didn't smile.

"What d'ya mean by that?" Wiley asked, exactly the same as before.

"Quit repeating yourself and let the man talk," Nest said.

"What d'ya mean by that?" Wiley asked, exactly the same as before. Nest shook his head in mock disgust, then turned to Buff.

"What d'ya mean by that?" Nest asked. Wiley snorted a laugh.

"Yup," Buff said. "She said he stole her and then she offered money to anybody who would carry her back home. 'Course, them not being no fools, none of the others did nothing on account of they didn't want to get shot. That Stacy killed one of them earlier, I guess." He turned and got the coffeepot and proceeded to fill their cups while they watched his every move. He set the pot on the bar and pretended to be thinking deeply.

"Let's see," he drawled. "Girl's name was . . . girl's name was . . ." He made them wait for a few seconds. "Yeah," he finally said. "Girl's name was Martha."

Fifteen minutes later, Buff shaded his eyes with a meaty hand and watched the two lawmen ride over the bluff to the north. He looked around carefully, scanning the horizon for signs of anyone else, but there was no one.

He had never seen a lawman act so surprised as that Nest fellow, with Wiley almost as shocked. Buff grinned now that there was nobody to see him. First time he could remember enjoying a conversation in years. He scanned the horizon again. Now where was that miserable Stubby Barnes and his jerkline team? Buff shook his head. He was going to have to go on short rations pretty soon if that no-good mule skinner didn't show up in the next day or so.

He turned to go inside, then stopped and looked to the north once more. He grinned and shook his head. What with Stacy and that girl, Jubil and his men hunting them, and two angry lawmen hunting them all, that particular part of the country was apt to get a mite crowded all of a sudden. He wasted a moment wishing he could be there to watch, then turned and went inside.

* * *

The smell of bacon cooking, buried in the scent of fresh coffee, worked into Martha's dream and slowly brought her awake. Stacy was hunkered down over the fire, fiddling with food cooking in a skillet. He looked over at her.

"Morning," he said. Martha suddenly realized the sun was peeking over the edge of the arroyo, which meant it was mid morning already. Stacy must've allowed her to sleep late. Guess he did know how bone-tired she was last night.

"Morning, Mr. Leech," she said back and rolled out of the bedroll. She was stiff and sore all over, and in spite of herself she could not hold back a small groan as she got to her feet. Stacy grinned over at her.

"Pretty soon you'll be tougher," he said with a friendly smile. "Couple more days in the saddle ought to do it." He was trying to be friendly, trying to put her at ease. Didn't seem right for her to glare at him that way.

"I don't expect to be with you for a couple more days," she snapped. "Matter of fact, I believe you will likely be dead by this time tomorrow or day after." He shrugged.

"Always a possibility," he said. He poured her a cup of coffee and she took it from him. It was pretty good as she sipped at it.

"Why don't you give this up," she said. "You can't want Nest this bad. Better the two of you should go your separate ways." Stacy piled bacon and pota-

toes on a plate, put two biscuits on top and handed it
to her. He held on to it for a second after she took it,
and they were only inches apart. He looked her right
in the eye.

"Don't care about Nest," he said. "Got no interest
in him whatsoever." He let go. Martha sat down, took
her fork and began to eat.

"I don't understand," she said as she chewed. "If
you don't want to kill Nest, why did you take me?"
His level gaze bothered her as the silence dragged out.

"I wanted you," he finally said, very softly.

Martha felt her eyes open wide in surprise and she
stopped in mid-chew. Never had she been more
shocked in her whole life. It was almost too much to
take in at once. How could she have been so wrong
about him? She finally began to chew again as she
thought about the new turn of events.

"Me?" she asked. "You want me?"

"Yup." Plain and straight.

"I don't understand." And she didn't understand.
How could this man she had never seen before last
week suddenly decide to steal her away? And why?
Surely he never thought she would like being stolen,
like being taken away from the only family she had
known for a long time. Surely he didn't expect to get
away with it.

"I was back in town on account of Mom died and
I had to settle up her affairs," Stacy explained quietly.
Martha was shocked. He must mean Old Marion, who

was sort of the character of Fleet. She had made her living doing folks' washing and finding old bottles that she cleaned and resold to the saloon and the store. Martha had never even considered that the toothless old woman had been a mother.

"I saw you walk to the general store the first day, and I have to admit I was took. I never felt anything like it before, only I knew that you were the only woman for me, knew that we were supposed to spend the rest of our life together." He looked sheepish, with his eyes down to the fire. He was baring his insides, laying himself vulnerable before her.

"I took the room so I could be close to you. I figured in a month we could get to know each other and you would learn about me and maybe I'd have a chance to make you my own, good and proper." He sighed. "Nothing is ever neat and easy about living," he said. "Nest showed up and I had to leave before I could convince you of how charming I was." He grinned and looked up at her. He looked so much like a little boy when he grinned, that she had to smile a little.

"Why did you have to leave just because Nestor showed up?" Martha asked. Much to her surprise, she discovered her plate was empty. He reached for it and filled it once more. He filled one for himself too. It gave him a chance to think about his answer.

"I am a wanted man in this state," he said. "I am not proud of it, and I did not do anything other than defend myself, but regardless of the reason, I am wanted. Only reason Nestor and I didn't have at it right then and there was on account of I was staying in his home and I had just saved your honor right in the middle of town.'' Martha thought about that while she ate.

''You thought I'd forgive you for stealing me away?'' she asked, disbelief clear in her voice. He sighed.

''I didn't have time to think it through,'' he said. ''If I had, you wouldn't be dressed in my clothes, you'd have your own.'' They ate in silence for a minute.

''I am not a bad man, Martha, not really. I meant you no harm. Quite the opposite, in fact. I want to take care of you and keep you from harm.'' He sighed again and she could tell how hard it was for him to talk about his most secret feelings. This big man was revealing his softness inside to the one person who could hurt him the most. In a way she couldn't help but be flattered. He went on.

''I could not bear the thought of not seeing you each and every day. So I stole you.'' She said nothing.

''If you give me a chance,'' he said desperately, ''if you take the time to learn a little about me, maybe you won't see me as this evil man who stole you away.'' He straightened and shrugged. ''It's not my fault, really. I couldn't help myself. It's actually kind of your fault.''

"My fault?" she asked, surprised.

"Yup," he said. "If you just weren't so pretty, you could still be back there cookin' and cleanin' for all those folks instead of out here having all this fun and adventure." She laughed, just as he had intended.

"Fun and adventure, huh?" she said. "Tell me, Mr. Leech, just what were your plans from here? We going to be on the lam forever? Going to rob banks and trains? What did you have in mind?"

"I told you I am not an outlaw," he said a little petulantly. "I already told you what my plans were. We are going to my ranch up in Montana. It isn't much yet, but it is built good and if we work hard together, we can make it into something."

"You really have a ranch?" She was surprised again. Seemed like this big man was full of surprises. He grinned at her, his boyish grin, and shrugged.

"Like I said, it isn't much, but it is mine and I got it legal and worked it hard already."

"And the law would just leave you alone up there, huh?"

He shrugged again. "I am not wanted for anything in Montana," he explained. "Up there, I am a good citizen and known as such in the town. Town isn't much either," he said with that boyish grin. "Will be someday, though."

Stacy suddenly stiffened, and in a second Martha heard it too. The flat cracks of distant gunfire, very faint. Stacy kicked at the fire, scattering the coals, and poured the remaining coffee on them.

''Clean up the camp,'' he ordered as he snatched her saddle from the ground and headed for the horses.

Just like that, the mood changed from calm and peaceful to hurried and serious. Martha asked no questions, just started packing the dishes and food away, helping Stacy get ready for their flight if need be. She came across her gun belt lying on her side of the bedroll, and took a second to strap it on. Not that she figured on ever using it, just that it was easier to wear it than pack it.

She finished rolling up the bedroll and stopped for a second to listen. It seemed like the shooting was getting closer.

Stacy came back for the second saddle and saddled up his horse. He left the two horses' reins hanging down, ground-tied, they called it. The horses were trained not to move while ground-tied. He slid his Henry from its sheath, levered a shell into the chamber, and slipped another shell through the loading gate. He was as ready as he could be for whatever was to come.

Jubil looked around, unhappy. Everything seemed normal, his men were trailing along in the usual sloppy way, only something *felt* wrong. He couldn't see anything he could put his finger on, it was just that old familiar feeling he used to get during the war.

Something was wrong. They were in danger from something or somebody. He could tell Reb felt it too, because he had loosened his rifle in its sheath and checked that his pistol was secure.

He wasn't moving real fast, just following along that couple's trail, headed North. He figured on giving them another day at least before they took them. Going to be trouble with Webb when they had the woman, for sure. He vowed he would not let anything bad happen to her. 'Course if that man Leech had really stole her, plenty bad had probably already happened.

His horse snorted nervously and Jubil reached forward and patted her on the neck.

"Me, too," he said.

He heard the familiar buzz as a slug went past his right ear, followed immediately by a low grunt from Webb. Jubil had heard that sound so many times he did not have to turn to see that Webb had been hit hard by the bullet.

All of a sudden they were running flat out, racing hard across the rolling prairie. They had their six-guns out, banging away at who knows what as they raced away from the danger.

Finally Jubil saw them. Indians, Sioux probably, running parallel to their track just out of gun range. There were maybe twenty of them and he could easily see several of them waving rifles. Somehow Webb had managed to stay on his horse, pounding along with the rest of them, although the pain kept him bent over in the saddle.

Jubil's gun banged a couple of times as he loosed two shots at the Indians. He didn't figure on hitting any of them. He was just hoping to convince them to keep their distance. Much to his surprise, one of them threw up his arms and flopped from his horse, rolling over and over until the long grass swallowed him up. The other Indians moved slightly away from the running white men, but continued to keep pace. Jubil thought on it and figured they were trying to run out the white men's horses and then take them one by one. He had to find a place to hole up. Too bad about Webb. He wasn't much of a man, but Jubil could have sure used his skill with a gun. He looked for an arroyo where he could set up a defense.

It hadn't taken the Indians long to change Jubil's hunting party into a hunted party.

Chapter Eleven

Wiley hunkered down and studied the ground.

"Uh-oh," he said. Even Nest could see the signs of many horses.

"Unshod," Wiley added. So there. Indians. The whole order of priorities was suddenly changed. Now nothing mattered except Stacy and Martha. Jubil and his boys were forgotten.

"We have to catch up with them," Nest said. Wiley swung up on his horse.

"Yeah," he said. "Maybe the Indians won't find them. That Stacy seems to be a pretty good man out here." Nest grunted.

"Maybe," he said. "Let's go," and he booted Rusty into motion. He hoped they wouldn't be too late, although he didn't really see how it would do much good to be on time. Wasn't too much three men and a woman could do against twenty angry Sioux.

The signs of twenty horses were easy enough to follow, and they settled into that ground-eating canter. The horses could keep that pace for quite a while. Maybe they would be in time to help. Nest patted his pistol and checked to be sure his Henry was still safe in its sheath. Maybe they would be in time.

They could easily hear the pounding of horses running hard, and Martha looked at Stacy, fear plain on her face.

"What is it?" she asked. He shook his head, rifle ready in his hands.

"Don't know," he said. "Some kind of running fight, I'm thinking. Indians, maybe." He glanced over and saw her eyes widen.

"It is good to be scared," he said, "only don't get too scared. If we have to fight, you remember what I said about using the gun. Aim for the middle and squeeze the trigger. Doesn't hurt to get a little bit mad, either."

"Fight?" she asked. He was pleased to see she had herself under control once more. "Are we going to have to fight?" She pulled the heavy pistol from its holster. He smiled over at her and she was surprised at how much comfort she took in that little smile.

"First we'll just try to disappear," he said. "If something isn't moving out here, it can be mighty hard to see, especially when you are riding hard on a horse.

Maybe if we just stay still, they will ride right on by.''
He took off his hat and looked over the shelf, rifle
ready, waiting to see what life had in store for them.
Martha moved next to him, pistol hanging heavy at
her side. They looked at each other for a moment, eyes
locked, then the pounding of hooves drew their eyes
toward the open end of the arroyo.

The Indians split off to the right, and the four men,
their quarry, split off to the other side. It appeared as
though they were going to be right in the middle.

''Don't look right at them,'' Stacy warned. ''Don't
catch their eye,'' and he was still, rifle lying on the
grass in front of him. Martha looked straight ahead,
ignoring the urge to look up and see the savages. The
pounding hooves got closer very fast, and suddenly
there they were, only a few feet away, running hard.
Clumps of earth were thrown into the air by the
horses' hooves, and one of them fell and hit Martha
right on top of the head. She jerked in surprise and
looked up.

The last Indian in line snapped his head in her direction, eyes caught by the movement almost under
his feet. Then he was past, running hard, and she
thought he had not seen her. She watched the Indian
straighten and pull his horse to a stop. He sat there for
a moment, still as a statue, and she heard Stacy's voice
real low.

''Keep going, Indian,'' he said. ''You didn't see

anything. Keep going with your friends.'' But the Indian turned his horse and came walking back.

He was really magnificent, tall and straight, and she could easily see the vermilion lines painted on his face. His skin was a dusky red and he was altogether a handsome figure as he rode his spotted horse back to the arroyo. He had a rifle in his hand, and he brought it up to a ready position as his eyes searched the edge of the bank for what he thought he had seen before. He was riding directly toward them.

Martha jumped and screamed as Stacy's rifle crashed right beside her, and the unseen bullet smashed into the Indian's chest and flipped him right off the back of his horse. Stacy looked over at her and gave her a tight little smile.

''Maybe they didn't hear that,'' he said. He shook his head and looked faraway for a moment. ''I sure hate to kill a man straight out like that. He had no chance whatsoever.'' He worked the lever and slipped another shell through the loading gate.

''It was my fault,'' Martha said, almost more to herself than to him. ''Some dirt hit me and I looked up at him and he saw me.'' Stacy looked down at her and shrugged.

''He probably would have seen us anyway,'' he said. ''He was awful close.'' He grinned. ''Like to scared me to death,'' he added. Martha didn't smile back.

''Me, too,'' she said.

But the shot had been heard . . . by both sides.

Reb led his group in a circle, turning back to the arroyo they had just passed. It had to have been Leech and the girl. Only other white people out here far as he knew. That meant one more gun to help, if they could get back there alive. He hunched lower on his horse and flayed him with his spurs. He could see that the Indians were trying to cut them off, and he cocked his pistol. Three rounds left in the cylinder. They pounded toward the arroyo.

Martha and Leech heard the horses pounding closer. Their eyes locked for a moment.

''I'm sorry,'' Martha said.

''Me, too,'' said Stacy. He held her eyes for a long second, then turned away and raised his rifle. Martha thumbed back the hammer on the big gun and let it rest on the prairie in front of her.

''Aim at the middle and squeeze,'' he heard her mutter. He was very proud of her. Side by side, man and woman, they waited for what was to come. They were ready.

Reb's horse burst over the bank, sliding down in a cloud of dust, and suddenly there was noise and dust and confusion everywhere. Jubil and Amos were right behind, horses sliding and snorting in fear and exhaustion.

The Indians were coming directly at the V of the arroyo, and the three newcomers pressed up against the bank on the left side while Stacy and Martha were on the right. Howling war cries, the Indians thundered down on the small group.

Stacy rested his arms on the edge and sighted on an Indian. His rifle slammed back and the Indian disappeared, thrown off his horse by the heavy slug. He worked the lever and picked another target. This one was almost directly on them when the rifle crashed again, and he too was down and broken.

The Indians split at the V like water before the prow of a ship, sweeping down both sides of the arroyo and off into the prairie. In a moment they were gone. Stacy turned his head to look at the three men.

"Howdy," he said.

"Nice to see you again," Jubil answered. Stacy smiled.

"I believe you might mean that," he said. Martha was amazed. These two men were in desperate danger, yet they were carrying on a conversation in a tone that would not have been out of place in the parlor. Stacy slipped a couple more shells into the Henry, and Jubil opened the gate on his rifle, blew it out and reloaded.

"You get any there?" Jubil asked.

"Two down," from Stacy.

"I got one," Jubil said.

Reb shook his head without looking away from the prairie.

"Missed mine," he said. "He moved." Amos cackled at Reb.

"You want I should go out there and hold 'em still fer you?" he asked. Reb ignored him.

"Now what?" Martha asked Stacy softly. "Are they gone?"

"Nope," he said. "They'll circle around and get together first. Then if their blood is still hot, they'll come at us again. If they're thinking instead of feeling, they'll probably try to work out some strategy to smoke us out or wait us out or maybe pick us off one by one." Her face fell as she looked up at him.

"But they're not going to give up, are they?" He smiled on her tenderly.

"They might if we can kill them all, or at least enough so they figure their medicine is bad. So far we put down four of them and they didn't get any of us."

"They got one of us," Jubil said. Stacy took that in and nodded.

"If I can figure right," Stacy said, "that makes a rate of four of them for every one of us. Guess we should run out of Indians just about the same time we run out of us." Jubil looked across at him and grinned, the first time Martha had seen him smile.

"Somehow, that sounds most unsatisfactory when you say it that way," he said. He turned back to the prairie. "If they're going to come again, it ought to be pretty soon," he added, almost to himself. He pulled back the hammer on his rifle and peered out into the tall grass.

The five of them lay there like that, senses straining

out into the waving grass, for almost an hour. Martha was a little disappointed in herself. The first charge had come so fast, so confused, that she had not even fired her big pistol. It lay on the prairie under her hand, ready for action, but so far unused.

She was loath to kill a fellow human being, but it seemed cut and dried. The Indians or her and Stacy. Reduced to its simplest terms, the solution was obvious and she vowed the next time she would not hesitate or be disoriented. She suddenly became aware that the old man had turned and was staring at her.

"Missy," he said as he wiped his mouth with the back of his hand. "Since we're going to die here anyway, how about a hug for a lonely old man." He sniffed wetly and tried to look piteous. Jubil rolled to one side and looked at Amos.

"Amos," he said softly. "If the Indians don't kill you, I will. Turn around to the front and if you so much as speak to that young lady again I will kill you on the spot." Amos looked surprised, then hurt, his face wrinkled up until it almost looked like he was going to cry.

"Aww, gee, Jubil," he said. "What's the harm? I mean, we're prob'ly goners anyhow." Jubil's hand moved toward his pistol and Amos held up a hand in fear.

"All right, all right," he said. He turned his gaze back out to the prairie. "Don't see why you get so riled up about something that don't mean nothin'," he mumbled just loud enough for all to hear, then settled into a hurt silence.

The first shower of arrows arrived with a fast whistling sound, then many thumps as they buried into the sides of the arroyo. Nobody was hit, but the horse Amos had been riding went to his knees without a sound, then flopped on his side, kicked futilely into the air a few times, and was still.

"Roll on your backs," said Stacy. "Keep watch on the other side of the arroyo and watch for arrows coming down. Might be we can see them coming soon enough to get out of the way."

They had no more flopped to their backs when Martha saw the next shower of arrows arcing down on them from high in the sky. One of them was coming directly at her, and she rolled to one side as the arrow thudded into the ground where she had been.

Amos fired his rifle, and Martha heard the slug whine over her head into the prairie. He reloaded and fired again and again.

"Stop shooting," Jubil said loudly. "They want you to waste your ammo like that. Wait until you see something."

Amos finished loading, pulled back the hammer and let fly another slug into the prairie.

"Stop it, Amos," Jubil said, louder. Amos turned his head toward Jubil.

"No!" he said. "I'm tired of listening to you, and

I'm sick and tired of them Indians out there. Maybe I'll hit one of them and they'll stay back.''

''You are not going to hit any of them shooting blind like that,'' Jubil said, and the next shower of arrows arced into the sky.

''Look out!'' yelled Stacy, and down they came, thudding into the ground. This time Martha didn't have to move. They all missed her, but she saw one of the little sticks hit Amos right in the stomach, down kind of low. She could easily hear him grunt.

After a moment of silence, Amos said, ''They got one into me that time.''

Martha was the only one who looked at him. The old man had a surprised look on his face as he looked down at the feathered stub protruding from his belly. He reached down and touched it experimentally, rubbing his thumb down the smooth edge of the feathers.

''I'll be,'' he said. ''Don't hurt none, least not yet.''

Jubil glanced over at him. ''It will,'' he said.

''Yeah,'' Amos agreed. He had seen men gut-shot before. He knew what was in store for him.

Stacy jabbed Martha in the side.

''Keep your eyes in the sky,'' he snapped, ''else you will wind up like him.'' Martha jerked her attention back into the sky, but she kept watching Amos from the corner of her eye. He laid there for a few minutes breathing normally, watching the sky. He kept feeling the arrow in an absent-minded way. Finally, he spoke.

"Well, boys," he said. "They have kilt me for certain. Only I am not going alone. I'll be seein' you," and he took his pistol in one hand, his big knife in the other, and crawled into the prairie and was shortly out of sight.

"He always was a feisty old varmint," Jubil said to nobody in particular. Silence fell over the group.

"Look out!" from Reb, and another arrow shower thudded into the ground. A quick check by Stacy showed no injuries this time, although Reb had to roll over quickly and was looking ruefully at the arrow stuck where he had been lying before.

"Never saw them do this before," Stacy said.

"Me, neither," from Jubil.

"Must have a new chief," Reb said. "Smart one, too."

"Too smart for Webb and Amos," Jubil said.

An awful scream split the quiet, and Martha jumped. Stacy reached out and patted her on the shoulder.

"Easy, girl," he said. "That was an Indian. Likely Amos got to him."

There was another scream that cut off suddenly. Nobody said anything. They had all recognized the voice.

"They are still maybe two hours ahead of us," Wiley said as they rode. "We are likely gaining on them a little, 'specially if we keep going at this pace." He reached down and patted his horse's neck. His hand came back flecked with foamy sweat, but the horses were still going strong.

"We can only go like this a piece further," Nest came back. "Then we will have to slow down or risk walking."

"I know," said his friend, and they rode across the prairie, each lost in his own fears of what they would find when they finally did catch up with their quarries.

Yellow Knife couldn't say exactly how he had become the leader. The others had wanted to rush right at the white men again and he had stepped one step forward and held up his hand and the others had fallen silent.

"To rush into their guns when they are waiting for us is foolish," he said. "More of us will die, and for what?" He looked at the others. He still had their attention. "They are trapped," he said simply. "If we put one or two of us at the open end of the gap in the earth, the white men cannot escape. We can shoot at them from in the grass and maybe kill some of them. Sooner or later the others will tire of the fear and will surrender to us. We can take their horses and weapons without any more of us being killed." There was silence while the others thought that over.

"What do we do with them after they have surrendered to us?" asked Crooked Fist.

"Kill them!" barked White Feather. The others grinned in agreement.

"We can kill them if that is your wish," said Yellow Knife, "but I think it is a bad idea. Killing them would be over in a short time and we would gain nothing. It might be better to take them with us and trade them back to other white men for weapons." He stood there and waited patiently while they thought that over.

"How do you want us to do this thing?" asked Crooked Fist, finally. Yellow Knife leaned forward and explained his plan.

It was only later, while he watched his planning come to life, that he realized he had become a leader. He was a warrior.

Chapter Twelve

Crooked Fist sighted down the barrel of the rifle Yellow Knife had given him. It did not occur to him that the rifle should have been his anyway because he had killed the mule skinner. No. It was Yellow Knife's rifle, and Yellow Knife had presented it to him and it was a thing to be truly cherished.

There was some kind of insect biting him on the side and he dearly wanted to reach down and squash it, but he remained motionless. Sooner or later that man who was his target would raise up or make some other stupid move and Crooked Fist would squeeze the trigger like he had practiced. Then there would be one less enemy to worry about.

Crooked Fist had not heard of others fighting in exactly the way Yellow Knife had told them, but when he thought about it, it seemed like a good idea. Besides, it was safer, and even though he was brave he did not wish to die any sooner than he had to.

He saw a movement ahead in the gap, but he still did not have a good target, so he waited. "Be patient," Yellow Knife had said. He would be patient. He wondered about the scream he had heard earlier.

A coyote barked out in the prairie, only Stacy knew it really wasn't a coyote. Another flight of arrows arced into the air and they all judged the flight of the projectiles. Martha rolled to her left and two arrows thudded into the ground where she had been. She never saw the second set coming, for they had been launched immediately after the first, intending to catch them unawares. They did.

Stacy grunted as one slammed into his left leg just above the knee. Reb shouted in pain as another embedded itself in his chest on the left side.

Martha looked at Stacy's leg with the feathered stick protruding from it. She couldn't believe it. He had been hit. He had been hurt. She stuffed the pistol back in her holster and rolled over by him. His face was pasty white and sweat beaded his forehead and upper lip.

"You're hurt," she said, then realized how foolish that sounded. "What can I do?" That was better. Now was not the time to let her emotions run away with her. Stacy touched gingerly at the wound.

"It goes all the way through," he said through gritted teeth. "Get something to use for a bandage." He stripped off his bandanna. "Here," he said. He rested against the bank and looked at her.

"What you have to do is break off the feathered end and pull the arrow out the bottom of my leg," he said. "Then wrap the bandage around the leg to stop the bleeding if you can." Martha studied the wound.

"Sure you don't want to just leave it in there for now?" she asked. "It isn't bleeding very much." He shook his head.

"I do not want that awful thing in there," he said. "Break it off and pull it out. Do it now. There may not be much time before they send in more arrows." His face was pale, but his voice was firm and so were his eyes.

"Okay, Stacy," Martha said. She could easily hear the wet gurgling of Reb trying to breathe on the other bank.

Jubil crawled over to Reb and immediately saw that the wound was fatal. His lung was pierced and flecks of red were coming from his open mouth with each painful breath. He was going to die soon, and Jubil would lose his only friend in the world. He already felt the hurt at the loss and Reb was not yet gone.

"Easy, friend," Jubil said, and he put his hand on Reb's shoulder. Reb looked at him through pain-filled eyes.

"It's over," he said. It was not a question.

"Yes," Jubil said. With much effort Reb put his hand on Jubil's shoulder.

"I am not sorry," he said. It was very hard for him to talk. "We were taking much and giving nothing back," he tried to explain. Jubil understood.

"I know," he said. Reb nodded. He gurgled two more breaths, then relaxed under his friend's hand and his hand fell from Jubil's shoulder to the ground.

Jubil pressed his hands against his face and rubbed vigorously as if trying to wipe away the loss of his friend. There was the sharp crack of a rifle from down the arroyo, and Crooked Fist's bullet went right through Jubil's hand. The body that had been Jubil sighed one last time and fell to the ground, finally at peace.

Martha took the feathered end of the arrow in her hand, feeling Stacy wince when she touched the wooden shaft.

"Hang on," she said, and snapped the end of the arrow off cleanly. He grunted in pain, and she forced herself not to hear him, but knew she would feel his hurt forever. She reached underneath, took the other end of the arrow and yanked it through as fast as she could. Stacy grunted again and dropped his head back against the bank. His eyes were closed and his teeth clenched in pain.

Hurrying as fast as she could, Martha wrapped the bandanna around the leg and tied it tight, pulling one

more groan from the injured man. She tied it in a knot
and looked up at his face.

His face was hard, jaw clenched under his white
skin. Beads of sweat covered his face, and almost
without thinking, she took off her bandanna and began
to pat the sweat from his face. He lay there for a moment, breathing hard, the feeling of her tender pats
driving back the dull pain. Finally, he opened his eyes
to her.

"It's okay," said Martha. She, too, was pale and
shaken. She tried a frail little smile. "It is all over
now." He gave her a wan smile in return, then his
eyes flicked past her and hardened. She turned slowly
and looked at all the Indian warriors standing on the
bank looking down at the only two survivors.

Wiley and Nest were walking fast, leading their
horses, still moving along the many tracks. Their
horses were covered with foamy sweat, and were
breathing hard. Intent on moving fast and also staying
alive if possible, the two men did not talk. Wiley
topped a small knoll and stopped suddenly. Very
slowly, very carefully, he eased back.

"Here they are," he said softly. He ground-tied his
horse, lay down in the tall grass, and crawled on his
belly to the top. Nest crawled up beside him. A mile
away, the single line of Indians rode toward them.

"They see you?" Nest asked.

"Don't think so." Nest took out his telescope and peered intently at the group.

"It must be all over," he said flatly. "I can see Stacy and Martha tied to their horses. They're tied together with a rope and the rope is tied to another Indian's horse." He studied the situation as the line of figures slowly rode closer. "Be kind of hard to get them out of there, I'm thinking," he said.

"How many?" Wiley wanted to know.

"Looks like fourteen," Nest answered. "It appears like Stacy has a bandanna wrapped around his leg. Martha looks okay."

"They appear to be comin' this way," Wiley pointed out rather unnecessarily.

"Yup," Nest agreed. He thought a moment. "We'll use the horses for cover and wait for them to come around the hill. They may be a bit careless just coming out of a fight like that, and with any luck they'll be under our guns before they know anything about it." He turned to his friend. "They'll probably figure you know how to shoot, too," he said. Wiley wasted a moment to glare at him, then slid back. He brought up the horses almost to the top of the hill and forced them down to their knees. He took a turn around their forelegs with a rope to keep them there. He and Nest got down between the horses side by side, resting their rifles on the saddle.

"I have been thinking on giving up this profession," Wiley said as he looked down the barrel of his

Henry, waiting for the Indians to appear. "I am not quite sure what profession I should get into, though," he went on in a conversational tone. "Any ideas?"

"You ever get the feeling you have been somewhere before?" his friend asked. "I'd swear we've done this before."

"Let's hope it ends up the same way," Wiley said.

"Yeah. Don't expect to see Rebecca come walking across the prairie this time, though." Nest was surprised at how the mere mention of her name affected him. He could almost see her, walking across the land, big pistol in her hand; could almost hear her last good-bye to him. "I want you alive," she had said. He knew he didn't want to die. He looked down the long barrel. Any second they should come riding around the hill.

"Worse comes to worst," Nest said softly to his friend, "I'll take out the Indian tied to them. Maybe they can get away while we fight them off."

"Okay," said Wiley. "I will take out the leader." "Sure you will," said Nest. "Remember, just put the little bead in the center of the notch and line them up with your target."

"Is that how you do it?" Wiley asked in a surprised tone. "I have been doing it all wrong up to now."

"No fooling," said Nest.

Wiley would have taken more pretended offense, but at that moment a single Indian rode around the hill and turned his horse to face them. He raised his right hand in a sign of peace. Nest and Wiley looked down their rifle barrels at the lone figure.

"Oh, for crying out loud," said Nest. "You track pretty good but you sure don't skulk well at all."

"Skulk?"

"Yeah, skulk. You are not very stealthy. They must have seen you from a mile away."

"Probably I should get a smaller hat," from Wiley.

"Hey," said Nest. "I believe I recognize that guy."

"Careful," said Wiley. "You know how they all look the same."

"Nope," from Nest. "That's him, sure enough." He rose to his feet and raised his right hand.

Yellow Knife was astonished to see the man called Nest. Never in his wildest imagination had he considered that he might know the white men behind the hill. He almost wanted to smile a greeting, but this was time for serious work. Trading was to be done. Or fighting.

He studied the position of the two whites and approved. They had command of all the land around from their position of height, and cover from the prone horses. There was no way the Indians could take the two men without taking heavy losses. It was information a warrior might be able to use later, if there was a later.

He motioned with his hand, and Crooked Fist led the two captives out beside him.

"These are the men who held me captive," Yellow

Knife said softly. Crooked Fist looked up at the two men, standing there casually, rifles in their hands. He almost felt like he knew them, too, so often had the story been told.

"Which is the one called Nest?" he asked.

"The one near the top of the hill," said Yellow Knife. They were talking softly.

"He does not go so near the top that I can shoot him from the other side," observed Crooked Fist.

"He is a warrior," said Yellow Knife. "He is not so stupid." Crooked Fist studied the two men looking down on them.

"We could attack them," he said. "I am not afraid." Yellow Knife looked at him.

"It is not a matter of being afraid," he said. "They have repeating rifles. They could easily kill us all before we could kill them. Being brave does not mean that we must be stupid." Crooked Fist could see the sense in that, so he remained silent.

Yellow Knife made signs with his hands, signs that anyone could understand. The captives in exchange for the repeating rifles.

"Well, I'll be," said Wiley. "That is one unusual Indian, to my way of thinking."

"Might be we have a chance to get out of this alive," Nest said back. "Only I hate to let them have a good Henry rifle."

"They are likely to get these rifles one way or the

other,'' Wiley pointed out. ''Frankly, I prefer a nice friendly trade.''

Nest grunted agreement. He held up one finger and pointed to his rifle. One rifle, he was saying.

''Wonderful,'' said Wiley. ''Let's bargain. I can already feel my hair getting loose.''

Yellow Knife held up two fingers. Both rifles. Nest shook his head. No. There was a long pause while both sides pondered on the deal.

''I figure we can give them your rifle and never miss it,'' Nest said to Wiley. In spite of the situation, Wiley smiled.

Yellow Knife finally nodded. It was a trade. Better to have one repeating rifle and all of his braves alive, than two rifles and no braves. Or maybe no rifles and no braves. He took up the lead rope and led the two captives' horses up the small hill. Crooked Fist watched in silence.

Yellow Knife reached down with the lead rope and handed it to Nest. Wiley held up his rifle. Yellow Knife looked at it and shook his head. No. He nodded at Nest's rifle. Nest studied him for a moment, then handed his rifle up to the Indian. Yellow Knife took the weapon in his hand and felt the weight of it; the smoothness of it. He nodded. The trade was finished. He rode back down the hill, joined Crooked Fist, and they rode around the hill and out of sight.

Nest looked up and smiled. ''Hello, Martha,'' he said. Wiley cut her loose and helped her down. He pulled Stacy down where he collapsed to the ground with a grunt of pain. Wiley ignored him and left his wrists tied.

"No need to treat him that way," Martha said, heat in her voice. Wiley looked at her, surprised. She turned away from him. "Nice to see you, Nestor," she said with a big smile. He grinned.

"I expect you mean that," he said. He looked again. Sure enough, the Indians had not taken her pistol. He looked at her and raised his eyebrows in question.

"They thought it was funny," she said. "They actually laughed at me."

"Does look a little bit strange," he admitted. He hesitated, wondering how to ask. Finally, "You all right?"

Martha looked at her rescuer. She wanted to tell him about the days of hard riding, the worry, the wondering, the awful time at Beaver Station. She wanted to tell him about the horrible fight with the Indians and the sights and sounds of men dying.

"I'm all right," she said. Nest took her in his arms and hugged her to him, warm and safe. She smelled the man smell of hard days in the saddle, felt the warmth from him, and for the first time in days began to relax. Nest was here. She was safe now.

"How's our prisoner?" Nest asked over her head.

"He'll live," said Wiley coldly. "Long enough to hang, anyway." Martha stepped back. Nest was watching the line of Indians as they went away from them. Yellow Knife was still being careful not to bring his men under their guns, but he needn't have worried.

"That guy's going to be a great chief someday, I'm thinking," Nest said.

"Yeah," said Wiley as they watched them ride away. "Don't suppose they'll double back, do you?" Nest thought about that for a moment.

"Nope," he said. "I think we're a done deal, far as he's concerned."

"Wonder what his name is?" from Wiley. Nest grunted in reply. What could he say?

"Hang him?" asked Martha.

"What?" from Nest.

"He said they were going to hang him." She indicated the seated form of Stacy.

"Not a doubt in the world," said Nest.

"He has a ranch in Montana," she said. Nest looked at her, surprised.

"I hope he left it in good hands," he said. She looked upset.

"Nestor," she said. "Let him go."

"What?"

"Let him go," Martha repeated. "He did good by me when he didn't have to. He saved my life more than once. Let him go," she asked. "Please." Nest looked confused.

"I can't let him go, Martha," he said. "I'm a lawman. He's a wanted man, and I haven't even figured out how many laws he broke when he stole you."

"Can't you forget that for just a minute?" she asked. "I'm telling you, he's not a bad man. Please let him go."

Nest looked distressed.

"I'd like to, Martha," he said. "Really. I just can't. He's going back with us." His tone had a note of finality. She dropped her eyes and nodded. She looked over at Stacy, who was sitting there watching her. His eyes looked larger because of his paleness. Martha looked back at him for a long moment, then looked away.

Wiley helped Stacy get back up on his horse, and finally the big man was up there, comfortable in the saddle, or at least as comfortable as he could be with his hands tied to the horn.

Nest helped Martha mount her horse. He was absolutely flabbergasted when he went to smile up at her and stared instead in the black eye of her forty-five.

"Turn him loose," she said softly. Nest was absolutely speechless. "Turn him loose," she urged once more. "Let him go and we will leave your state and never come back."

"Wha . . . what?" was the best he could manage. He could see Wiley watching, wide-eyed. His expression was almost comical, and Nest realized his was probably the same.

"I . . . I like him," she tried to explain, tone earnest and pleading. "I don't want to see him hung." Nest recovered somewhat.

"Look, Martha," he said. "I am not going to let him go and that's final." He raised an eyebrow at her. "You don't really expect me to believe you are willing to shoot me, do you?"

Nest watched the cylinder turn as she pulled back the hammer, slowly. He could easily see the rounded shapes of the lead slugs.

"Nestor," she said softly. "Don't ever get between a woman and her man unless you are prepared to lose. Nest looked up at this woman he thought he knew. He looked at her for a long time. Then he smiled a small little smile.

"Cut him loose, Wiley," he said.

Wiley and Nest swung aboard. Martha and Stacy were a hundred yards away, heading north.

"Why didn't you take that gun away from her?" Wiley asked. "Some lawman you are when you let a girl get the drop on you and don't do anything about it."

"You're the one with the rifle," Nest pointed out. "That's our prisoner escaping out there. Why don't you stop him?"

"Okay, I will," said Wiley, and he pulled his Henry from the boot. "Now, what was it you said? Line up the notch with the what and the target?"

"Oh, never mind." Nest feigned disgust. "You'd probably shoot me by mistake."

"What makes you so sure it'd be by mistake?" Wiley asked. Nest grinned at him, then turned back to the two diminishing riders. He and Wiley watched them for a few minutes, then Nest took a deep breath.

"Well," he said. "Wonder what Ma's planning for supper day after tomorrow."

"Don't know," said Wiley. "Maybe I could shoot something on the way back." They turned their horses and started the long ride back to Fleet.

"We don't want to eat your horse," Nest responded.

"Now, there you go again," Wiley came back in a hurt tone. "Why, if I had a nickel for every time my shooting skill has saved your miserable life . . . " and the voices of the two friends slowly faded. A bee buzzed by in the sunlight. On the northern horizon, two riders slowly disappeared in the waving grass.